WARRIOR KING

THE CRYSTAL KINGDOM: NEW WORLDS

MILLY TAIDEN

WARRIOR KING

THE CRYSTAL KINGDOM: NEW WORLDS

NEW YORK TIMES and USA TODAY
BESTSELLING AUTHOR
MILLY TAIDEN

ABOUT THE BOOK

Lilah McClure may be mouthy, bossy, and overly bold, but she knows what's fair and hates injustice of any kind. When she and her cousins are captured by the mountain fae, she learns they're living in the freakin' stone age. Equality between genders? Nope, not even as a joke. The female fae need a champion to stand up for them against their king, show them how their lives should be free from oppression. Lilah is more than willing to take on that job. There's just one big, sexy, problem. Ferrus.

Ferrus sees no issues with how things have been for centuries. His beautiful, strong, independent woman is making him question the norms and traditions he's known all his life and wonder if maybe their society is in need of an update. He isn't sure what to believe, but he's fallen for this strange little human, so he'll do his best to keep her from being thrown into the dungeon, or eaten by wild forest creatures.

Lilah has to negotiate with a cold-hearted king for the future freedom of generations of females and show the fae she loves that his ways are barbaric and must change. We can't forget that some guy wielding dark magic is after her and her cousins, wanting his own revenge on the Crystal Kingdom.

Published By
Latin Goddess Press
Winter Springs, FL 32708
http://millytaiden.com
Warrior King
Copyright © 2020 by Milly Taiden
Edited by: Tina Winograd
Cover: Jacqueline Sweet

—For My Readers

Thank you for your support

I hope you love the rest of the Crystal Kingdom: New Worlds Books.

CHAPTER ONE

She would not cry, dammit. She would not. She was a McClure. And they did not cry!

Lilah stood at the edge of the forest faes' new village, staring into the distance. Among the tree trunks, if she stood in the right place, she could glimpse the mountains they had to cross on their way to get home—Earth home.

She couldn't believe how screwed up the portal stones were. So much for magic being all-powerful and shit. It was cool that Wren could control tree roots to make chairs and tables and have limbs lift stuff off the ground. Her cousin must've had a lot of their Grandmom's blood in her. Why Wren never showed her magic on Earth was beyond her.

Then again, what could one gain from moving branches and roots? Unless they could dig up treasure, what was the point?

Yes, she was trying to think about anything except the reason she was in the shitty mood she'd been in the past several days. Wren finding a "mate" didn't help any. The one thing Lilah had yearned for her entire life, and her cousin had it. Went to show how unfair life was.

Boy, had she learned that. Lilah sniffled and dug the toe of her shoe into the soft dirt. She had to suck it up and realize that anyone with her body shape, a medium pear...okay, a large pear, would have a difficult time finding someone who would take the time to see the real her.

She bit down on her lip to keep the tears at bay. Dammit! Behind her, leaves crunched. Lilah pulled her shoulders back and took in a deep breath.

"Hey, Lilah. You ready to go?" Daphne stopped next to her.

Lilah hoped her cousin hadn't heard her sniffling. Then the nosy woman would be asking all kinds of questions, getting up in her business, thinking she was a drama queen. Fuck that.

"Of course I'm ready to go. Why do you think I'm standing here?"

When Daphne cringed at her harsh words, she felt even more like shit. Dammit. Lilah stepped forward. "Let's get this caravan on the road. I'm tired of having to eat only healthy crap." Plus, she hadn't had a cup of coffee in ages. That explained her slight headache for the second day in a row. Did this planet not have anything with caffeine?

"Hey, wait up," Wren called out. Finally, her cousin and the love of her life were finished saying their goodbyes to the clan. It wasn't like they couldn't come back. As long as Grandmom had the magical gemstones, they could come and go whenever they wanted. After this, she seriously doubted the old woman would let them within a mile of the portal stones.

"Lilah," Wren huffed, "do you even know where we're going."

Lilah swung around, finger-pointing toward their destination. "It's a little hard to miss a whole mountain range."

Wren's brows drew down, then her face softened. Oh, hell no. Lilah knew that expression. Right now, she couldn't handle pity from anyone. She turned and traipsed faster, trying not to trip on a root and fall on her damn face.

"Lilah," Wren called in a soft voice. Quick footsteps headed toward her. Shit. Wren came up to her side. Lilah slowed, realizing her ploy to not talk about her shitty emotional state wasn't happening. "I'm sorry I haven't been around much the last couple of days. Not being a very good friend…"

That was what her cousin thought she was angry about? Seriously? "Don't worry about it," she replied. "The villagers were more than accommodating. And the dirt wall your boyfriend made between you two and Daph and me when we slept kept your snoring to a minimum."

"I do not snore," Wren blurted. She looked over her shoulder. "Zee, do I snore?"

After a pause, he said, "I'm not sure. We haven't done much sleeping."

Oh my god. Now they had to rub it in that they were having sex, while she didn't even remember what it was. Yeah, she'd told them it had only been a couple weeks, but the truth was more like a couple years. If she wasn't so grumpy, she would've laughed at Wren's very red face.

You know, this was too funny to pass up, cranky or not. Lilah busted out into laughter. "Shit on a shingle, Wren. You should see your face right now. It's epic." Lilah leaned back then forward, slapping her leg. "Damn, that's hilarious." She looked back at Zee to see his face was totally serious.

Lilah let out a whooping guffaw. Oh god! Her stomach hurt from laughing so hard. It felt good to release what she'd pent up the past few days. She wiped tears off her cheek.

Face still resembling a tomato, Wren stomped to her mate and smacked him on the arm. "You're not supposed to say stuff like that," Wren whispered.

Zee glanced at Lilah, then back at Wren, and smiled. "Sorry, love. I forgot your culture is strange about sex and your bodies." Wren smacked him again and mumbled about men.

Lilah stepped over a downed log. *Let the love birds have their time together.* At least someone was happy and having sex. She sure as hell wasn't on either account.

All right. Enough of the fucking pity party already. Lilah was getting disgusted with her own mental whining. McClure women were strong and independent, no matter how sad the situation.

She snapped her fingers a couple times. "Come on, scary as hell kitty," she said, referring to

Xenos's sabretooth tiger form. "You're the leader here." The couple passed by her.

That was something else she couldn't believe. Her cousin's mate was a shifter who turned into a tiger with fangs the length of her arm. Not to mention the whole clan's magical ability with the land. Seeing dirt rise into a mound to sit on and watching seedlings grow before your eyes was freaky.

She wondered if there were dragon shifters on the planet. That would be over the top. She'd been hung up on dragons forever; she still had her stuffed animal from childhood. One eye was missing, and an arm had been chewed off by the dog, but she still loved it.

After a while, they finally reached the base of the mountainside, where the trees couldn't take root. The group stopped and looked over the forest they had just left. Lilah hadn't realized they had been hiking uphill. Her extra-thick thighs and ass handled it better than she would've thought.

The beauty was breathtaking. There was nothing but trees and sky for miles both ways. They had to be really high up to see so far. Squinting, she noticed far in the distance where the forest looked like hell had come to the planet. All burned; nothing but scarred tree trunks.

Her heart sank at seeing the devastation. She hoped that one day the creatures who set fire to the trees would get their asses kicked. They could've burned down half the planet with the dark magic fire.

Zee pulled Wren to him. She was staring in the same direction. He whispered, "In time, the land will heal." He kissed Wren on the head. Lilah turned away before jealous tears sprouted.

Zee led them along a dusty trail that zigzagged up to the dip between two peaks. Thank god the pathway wasn't over one of the higher locations. Hell, a couple of mountains topped out above the clouds. If that was the case, she would've turned around and become a permanent gnoleon tree villager. They sure as shit had some drool-worthy men, but none who struck her fancy.

Not having heard Daph in a long time, Lilah looked over her shoulder to make sure her cousin was okay. Guilt rolled through her. She shouldn't have been so mean to her cousin. She should apologize, but her pride couldn't take the shame of seeming weak.

Something at the edge of the woods moved.

Something larger than a critter. "What's that?" she asked, tilting her head toward the spot. Zee narrowed his eyes in that direction.

He suddenly tugged on her and Wren. "Come, we need to keep climbing. We have to get to the other side."

"What," Lilah asked. "What do you see?"

"A couple of kappy scouts. Black magic surrounds them. Something I've not seen before."

"Oh my god," Wren whispered, "they're the ones who set the wildfire. They're still looking for us?" Zee squatted, the girls doing the same.

"I'm not sure," he answered. "Over there," he pointed to an opening in the rocks. "It could be a cave we can hide in until they're gone."

Keeping low to the ground, they made their way to the opening in the rock and slipped inside. Lilah peeked out. "I don't think they saw us. They're walking along the edge of the woods. When they're out of sight, we can go."

"Ow." Zee smacked his bicep, pulled out a toothpick-like stick from his muscle, then fell to the ground. Wren was beside him in an instant.

The sound of pebbles sliding over rock turned her head. A huge male came out from farther inside the tunnel, followed by several more men.

He said, "I suggest that you remain where you are, trespassers." Swords left their sheaths with a fingernails-down-a-chalkboard scrape.

"Oh fuck," Lilah whispered. *This is so not good. But damn, that dude is huge.*

CHAPTER TWO

"**G**et your damn hands off me." Lilah wrenched her arm out of the guard's hold. He held a sword in his other hand. Where did he think she was going? The men marched her and her cousins down tunnels in the mountain, which equated to a maze. She would never find her way out of here.

Lilah glanced back. Daphne was behind her with her own sexy guard. Wren was behind Daph, holding Zee's dangling hand. Zee was unconscious from the dart that hit his arm, and several men carried him.

The tunnels had been dark until their tour guide lit a torch. The walls and ceiling were level and straight, but rough. If she dragged her hand over the wall, it would be scratched. The ground, though, was as smooth as a concrete floor. She wondered how many feet had traveled this path.

The tunnel finally came to an end as they stepped into a hundred-foot-high cavern the size of a mall parking lot. Groups of men were scattered, each cluster doing something different: hand-to-hand combat, sword fighting, push-ups, and other soldier training stuff.

Here and there, she saw non-military people darting around. These beings wore what looked to be a mud-brown sheet over their heads, like a ghost on Halloween. One of the covered turned to her, and she saw a beautiful woman's face peer at her. Were all the sheet-wearing folks women? It was a stark contrast to Xenos's females who barely wore anything to cover their bodies.

The guards led them around the perimeter, staying close to the stone wall. Looking up, Lilah noted many arched openings carved into the walls, lined side by side and up and down, several rows high. Another material-covered woman carried a torch as she walked past several arches then stepped into one.

The space didn't look very big in the fire's light. Lilah could see some items in the room but couldn't tell what they were. The woman placed her hand on the wall at the corner where the outside wall ended at the entrance. Then she *pulled the rock wall to the other side* like closing a sliding door or gliding a curtain over a wide window.

How the hell did the woman do that? They definitely were not human. Maybe a different kind of fae than the gnoleons who lived in the forest.

The sounds of grunting pulled her attention to the men gathered ahead. They looked to be warriors with thick heavy swords and round shields. Conan the Barbarian had nothing on these guys. Their every limb was toned to perfection with taut muscles and very little clothing to cover only their stuff. Yowzers, her panties were melting.

She squinted as she got closer to them. The light was brighter on this end of the cavern with more torches mounted on the wall. She glanced at the guard walking next to her. His skin tone was light red as if he had sunburned from staying on the beach too long with no sunblock.

That was interesting. The gnoleon forest fae were a chocolate brown like the soil their magic commanded. These had an eternal blush over their entire bodies. That must have meant these fae were different from their tree-dwelling friends. Shit, she hoped the two races weren't enemies.

Xenos, Wren's mate, had not said anything about mountain-living fae, friend, or foe. But the gnoleon's original old home had been two days' walk away. Perhaps the two races didn't know of each other. Great. Complete strangers. She wondered if they could talk their way out of this. At least she and her cousins weren't being hunted by a deadly animal here.

As she glanced over at the soldiers, one caught her eye. He was staring directly at her. He stood among the men who quickly noticed his attention had moved, and all looked at her as well. Feeling her face heat, she focused straight ahead toward another tunnel.

She felt his eyes on her, and her body grew hot. Her pussy tingled for the first time in a long time. The image of his face was implanted in her mind. She would never forget that clean-shaven jawline, those large dark eyes, and full lips. Seeing him in her mind's eye made her stomach flip. God, she felt like a teenager with a crush on a movie star.

The light suddenly dimmed as her group entered another rock tunnel. Goosebumps popped up on her arms as the air became cooler the lower underground they went. On Earth, deep caves held a temperature in the sixties. Hopefully, they would be out of here before they found out what the average temp was.

After descending a few more minutes, a room cut into the rock came into view. Stepping inside, they were greeted with thick iron bars. It looked like a jail cell, except there was no door. How were they supposed to get in—

The guard wrapped his hands around two adjacent poles and bent them apart like they were ropes hanging from the rock ceiling. Astounded, Lilah stood gaping. A shove from behind got her moving past the bars, into the holding cell. Daphne was on her heels while their captors carried in Xenos and dropped him on the floor against the wall. Wren bundled her mate to herself, his head in her lap.

The guard bent the poles back to their straight position, then turned, and they all left. After a moment of silence, Lilah said, "Well, this sucks."

"Agreed," Daphne replied. Clueless on what to do, Lilah sat next to Wren and her unconscious mate.

Wren whispered with tears in her eyes. "Why

would they want to hurt him?" She glanced down at the face on her lap. "We hadn't done anything."

Lilah scowled. "According to them, we were trespassing."

"Whatever," Daphne added. "Since when is a mountain private property?"

"You would be surprised," Lilah said. "There are claims for all kinds of places you would think would be public domain." In her line of legal work, she had seen a lot of crazy shit the law did and did not pass. Land claims being only the tip of the iceberg.

Wren brushed the hair from her mate's face. "Zee hadn't mentioned anything about crossing someone's land. I wonder if he knew about these people."

Well, at the moment, they were not getting an answer to that. Lilah studied the gnoleon. "Why would they knock out Zee?"

"Out of all of us," Daphne said, "he is the only one who could put up a fight."

Lilah shrugged. The three of them definitely didn't look threatening, especially to men as big as these guys. She let out a deep breath, thinking what the next step should be.

"Okay, if you two don't mind, I'll do all the talking," Lilah said.

Daphne sighed. "That would be good. I wouldn't know what to say. You're used to arguing all day."

Lilah's brow lifted. That didn't sound good. But her job did require her to *persuade* others to agree with her side of the case. Which at times actually could look just like an argument. She knew what her rights were. She had often reminded the opposing litigant of what she could and could not say in a court of law.

Even though her job title was "paralegal," she had enough experience to open her own office to advise clients. She knew the laws and historical court cases like she knew the alphabet. The only thing lacking was a piece of paper, with a prestigious college name to hang on the wall.

CHAPTER THREE

"Watch for the dagger to your gut," Ferrus yelled at his men in training. Many years had passed since he and his people were threatened. Having a battle had been even farther in the past. He had a long way to go to get his men ready to fight, and they didn't have time—a couple days at the most.

"Prince Ferrus." His scout entered the cavern and knelt before him.

"Stand. Freedom to talk. What did you see?" Ferrus had sent out several scouts in the last few days to spy on the approaching enemy.

Scout answered, "They are the tree-dwelling fae from the Gecire forest, sire. Their magic grows plants they eat, and they control the ground to form into things."

"How many weapons do they have?" he asked.

Scout lowered his head. "Sire, I saw no weapons. They must be hiding them underground."

"I agree." Ferrus had no other idea why a village would move except for planning an attack to take more land. He would not give up his mountain willingly. He would fight to the death to protect his home.

"Anything more?" he asked his man.

"No, sire. Well, I did see something out of the ordinary…"

"Report," Ferrus barked.

The scout cringed from the exacting command. "Kappies were roaming the base of the mountain along the tree line."

"Why would kappies be this far from their caves?"

"I don't know the answer, Prince." The scout bowed low.

He waved away the soldier. "I did not mean for you to have an answer. Go on to the eatery. Come back when ready."

"Yes, sire." The scout rushed away.

How strange. Not only had the gnoleon arrived, but also creatures that were not customary in the region. He would speak to his father, the king, about this later. As prince and leader of the warriors, it was his responsibility to protect the king and glorify his name.

"Soldiers," he called out, "switch to hand-to-hand combat." He walked through the groups observing techniques and weaknesses. His men were warriors. The citogen were known for their strength and dexterity with a sword. Many of his men had been hired for security and guarding in the town and other places.

No one was a match for his troops. They could take down any enemy force, including the weak, peace-loving tree warts.

Ferrus stood with his men, observing when a weird feeling came over him. The animal inside him popped its head up, sniffing the air, going to full alert. But it wasn't warning him of danger. It was warning him of...mate?

Mother of the Mountain, this wasn't possible. It couldn't be possible. He looked up and saw his outer perimeter guards bringing in three females in strange clothing. The one with light hair grabbed hold of his insides and squeezed. She turned her head and locked onto his eyes.

His chest tightened, not allowing him to breathe. She was the most beautiful female he had ever seen. And her body was gorgeous. Those thick thighs and plump ass were made for his gripping as he pounded in and out of her. His cock came alive for the first time in a long time.

He pivoted away from his soldiers when the guards and visitors entered the tunnel leading to the holding cells. He needed to calm down before someone noticed and asked questions. He glanced back to make sure he saw what he thought he did. Yes, the guards were carrying one of the enemies.

This would be a very interesting day.

He waited for the security men to return from the hold. He would have answers immediately. But he had to be careful not to show too much interest in the female. For her sake as much as his.

Ferrus summoned the leader of the sentinels as soon as the guard returned to the main cavern. "Tell me what you have found for us, Ailred."

"Sire, I'm not positive about the two light-skinned females, but the male and his female are gnoleon. No doubt."

"Were they spying?"

"I believe not, Prince. As soon as we saw the male, we subdued him with a toxin. They were in the north-facing cave hiding from someone."

That was the side of the mountain the enemy currently held camp. "Excellent work, Ailred. Any information on the females. They are…"

"Different, sire?"

"Yes, different is a nice way to say it. Return to your post until the midday meal."

"Yes, sire. Thank you, sire." Ailred and his group bowed and hurried out the main entrance that was ground level.

He would wait until after the next meal before dealing with their guests. The image of the beautiful female would not leave his mind. He had not been with anyone in a hundred sun peaks. He'd had no interest. But now that all had changed.

He shook his head and growled to himself. His men noticed his agitation and took a step back.

"I won't be shifting. Back to sparring. Get a new weapon if you must." The clangs and grinding of metal on metal filled the cavern again. The pile of broken swords and bent shields off to the side was becoming too much. More and more men threw them away after the blades cracked or chipped or their shields twisted by a beating from a sword. This had turned into a problem due to his men's growth over the years.

Hundreds of years ago, before Ferrus came of age, the citogen army was much weaker than now. The fae were smaller and less muscled. After he took over the military training, their militants were chosen from the largest and strongest children. They were taught from an early age how important it was to strike fear into the hearts of the enemy. Fear made a fae weak, easy to take down.

But with the processes he had implemented came new problems. One issue being the men grew too strong for the metal they mined in the pits. He would speak with their sword maker to see what could be done to strengthen the metal to keep it from breaking. Going into battle with such weapons would get them all killed.

His dragon brought the visual of the female into his head. Dragon balls! He didn't need that right now. He had to focus on his men's fighting ability for the upcoming war. The dragon disagreed and plastered the image to the front of his brain so that he would "see" her continuously. A rumble started deep in his chest.

The warriors remained in action but side-eyed

him. There was something to be said about ruling with fear. The men would fight harder if they were afraid of punishment from losing.

A rough-toned voice drew everyone's attention. "If you ever take your eyes off the enemy again, I will slice your balls off and throw them in the lava pit. Do you understand me?" Ferrus sighed. Silvo was his second-in-command, but he sometimes thought he was top fae. He had embraced the king's style of rule by an angry force.

The woman's face flashed in his mind. Fine, dragon piss. He grabbed the closest soldier. "Take proper covering to the cells for the females and send the translator. Have them come to the throne room as soon as possible. Not the gnoleons." The man hurried out of the cavern into one of the various tunnels encircling the main room.

"Rest," Ferrus yelled, the echo going on and on and on. "I will return shortly. We have visitors to welcome."

CHAPTER FOUR

Sitting on the floor of the jail cell, Lilah rubbed her hands over her arms, trying to stop the goosebumps crawling over her skin. Wren still had Xenos's head in her lap, and she appeared unaffected by the chill.

"How long do you think they will keep us in here?" Daphne asked, pulling her arms inside her shirt to keep warm. That was a good idea. Unfortunately, her blouse wouldn't allow her to do that.

"They cannot keep us here forever," Lilah said. "We have rights."

"On Earth," Wren reminded her. "Who knows about here."

"Shouldn't matter where you are," Lilah argued.

"It is wrong to hold someone prisoner without giving them their say, period."

"Well spoken, young lady."

Lilah jumped to her feet and approached the man coming through the entrance. Wrapping her hands around the bars, she glowered at him. Most men scurried away when she flashed this side of her.

"I demand that—"

The guy shoved brown fabric at her and tossed another toward Daphne.

"Females, I am the translator. You will speak to the king through me. Please properly cover yourself."

Lilah let the material drape from her fingers. It was her own ghost sheet. She quickly pulled it over her head and bundled in it for warmth. Now she understood the need for covering up.

Daphne said from the rear of the cell, "Why don't you have one for Wren?"

The translator sneered at the couple on the floor. "They will remain here. There will be no spying on our troops."

A man dressed in the same attire as the soldiers came forward and gripped the bars, bending them open for Lilah and Daphne to step out.

"What do you mean 'spying'?" Daphne asked. "Spying for what?"

The guard pushed Daph and her behind the translator. Guess they wanted them to follow the guy. He could have just asked. Now that she had adjusted to her surroundings, she took the opportunity to study the area more. The more she knew about these people and their culture, the better she could tailor what she said.

The tunnel floor and walls weren't smooth. This passage didn't look as worn down as the others they came in through. That told her that this passage wasn't used a lot, meaning they hadn't imprisoned many others over the years. But the tunnel continued past the holding cell into complete blackness. There were no mounted torches like in the big area. She wondered if something important could be hidden farther down.

At an intersection, they turned down a tunnel she hadn't seen before.

"Hey, translator," Lilah said, "where are we going exactly?"

Without turning, he said, "We are going to the throne room. The prince has requested your presence before the king."

"Prince, huh?" she said, thinking about the

drop-dead gorgeous guy she saw when they came in. It was unlikely that he was royal. He was a soldier, obviously, but there was something about him that made him stand-out from the others. Something made him different, a little bit "more." She would so willingly let him eat crackers in her bed anytime. As long as she was on his list to eat too.

No, no, no. Those thoughts had to wait until they were out of this mess. This was serious, and they could find themselves locked up here until their bones turned to ash. That did not sound appealing.

Turning another corner, they stopped at a set of double stone doors. Etched into the front of each one was a huge dragon-like creature. Not one with wings, but more Godzilla-ish to move easier across on the ground. Seeing how much she loved dragons, these were stunning. She wondered if there really were dragons here or if they were a myth like on earth.

The translator slipped behind the doors while the guard in the rear of the group stood over them. Lilah glanced over her shoulder and caught him checking her out. His eyes lit up with lust as his look raked down her body again. What the hell?

She was covered head to toe in a sheet. What did he see?

Even though she was flattered that he liked her pear form, the creep sent chills down her back. He didn't compare to her soldier. She gave a polite turn-up of the lips and faced the doors.

The translator came back and whispered, "The prince and king are here for your questioning. I remind you to speak through me."

"You mean we give you our answers, and you will translate for us, right?" Lilah asked. She understood this process. When in court, the clients talked with her and not the judge directly. There was more order that way.

The doors opened fully this time, allowing them entrance. The throne room was not what Lilah expected. Not that she'd seen a lot of them. Bare stone walls and floors with a shiny, metal, grandiose throne in the center. No other furniture or rugs. Absolutely no female touches. Where was the queen? Surely, they'd let the royalty decorate the place.

She didn't see the prince either. The corners of the room were pitch black. Anybody or anything could've been creeping along the wall back there. Their translator stopped several feet in front of the old man in the gaudy chair. He bowed low. "My King, may I present our guests."

Lilah let out a snort that echoed in the room. Oops. But saying they were *guests* was a bunch of BS.

The king looked at the guy standing before her. "Who are these people, and why were they trespassing?"

The magic that interpreted all words into one universal language worked fine. Lilah understood the old guy perfectly. Why did they need a translator?

The translator turned back to her. "Who are you, and why were you trespassing?"

Somewhat confused, Lilah answered to him. "We are passing over to the other side. We were hiding in the cave when your people took us by force."

Their guide turned to the king. "Sire, they are travelers who took shelter in our cave to conceal themselves."

The king nodded, his brows drawn down tightly. "I have not seen fae the same color as your skin. What clan are you from?"

Their man turned to her. "The king has not seen fae the same—"

Lilah sighed, rolling her eyes. What was up with this stupid shit? She slid sideways and looked at the ancient dude. "We are—"

"SILENCE!" The king yelled, jumping to his feet. The translator got in front of her, waving his hands before her face, shushing her.

"Stop it," Lilah told him. "Get out of my face."

"I said silence!" the king repeated.

"I heard you the first time." Lilah said but looked at the "decipherer" while she said it.

The translator leaned into her face. "Talk to only me. You are not allowed to speak to His Highness."

"Why am I not allowed to speak?" Oh right, she'd forgotten he was her *lawyer,* and she was the client who was supposed to be quiet in front of the judge. But why was he repeating what the king said? She wasn't deaf.

The translator's eyes popped wide to her question. He gave her a look like he could not believe she had asked such a question. "For the same reason you must wear the coverings. You are female."

Whoa. Hold the fucking door. He did not just say what she thought he said! Her eyes narrowed on him. Through clenched teeth, she ground out,

"Are you saying I cannot talk to the king because I'm a woman?"

"Correct."

Her injustice radar kicked into high speed. She heard Daphne chuckling behind her. Her cousin knew her rather well. And soon, all of these chauvinistic males would too. She propped her fists on her hips.

"So," she started loud enough for everyone to hear, "Mr. Translator, please ask the king, if I had a dick like you…" The men gasped; their interpreter's face went pale from its sunburn color. "…then I would be allowed to talk?"

Her guy swayed on his feet. She reached out a hand to steady him, and he yanked his body backward. "You are not allowed to touch a male."

Her brow raised. She had the feeling the women here were not allowed to do a lot of things that were God-given rights. Daphne cleared her throat loudly. Yeah, Lilah would get herself in trouble. One more smart-ass remark. "Let me make one thing clear for you and your *king*. Where we come from, the females let the men *think* they are in charge. Nobody tells us what we can and cannot do."

She fixed her eyes on the king's and pointed at

him. "And people like you and your kind were destroyed because you are too stupid to see how things really work."

The royalty's face became tomato red, and his hands balled into fists. "How dare you speak to me." His face twisted into scary anger.

Right, if he thought she was afraid of him, he was dead wrong. If she could handle the grumpiest, meanest, asshole-ish judge in Carrollton county, then this guy was ground meat. With quick, long strides, she was in the royal's face. Just to piss him off more and to make a point, she poked him in the chest with a red lacquered nail.

"I am not scared of you. I have dealt with so many of your kind in my job that I eat them for breakfast." That wasn't entirely true, but it sounded damn tough. "I demand that you release us to go on our way before somebody does something *you will* regret." She had always wanted to say that phrase. She had read it a hundred times in her romance novels, and it applied so well here.

The king stared down at her as his body began to shake, and his face got darker. Somebody had better do something before her bravado from being treated unjustly faded with her adrenaline.

Movement in the shadows caught the corner of

her eye. A body dashed out toward her. The frame was not any larger than hers, so she knew it wasn't a soldier coming to kill her. She didn't think they would really hurt her. Put her back in lockup, maybe.

Lilah didn't dare move her eyes away from the monarch. Her boss had taught her one thing in her first week on the job—don't let anyone intimidate you. Never look away first.

"Father, My King, let me take them and show them our ways, so they learn to be proper females."

Okay, this little surprise warranted looking away. So, the daughter of the king was allowed to speak to him, just not the commoners. Her indignation fired up again.

The king lifted his arm toward his daughter. "Go with her before I leave you in the dungeon with the spies to rot."

There was that *spy* word again. There wasn't anyone else in the cell with the four of them. In response to his order, she raised her chin.

"I *choose* to leave because this room disgusts me with its ugly hardness and irritating occupants." She reached out to Daphne and pulled her along. "Come on, Daph. We are so out of here."

The daughter ran toward an archway. Lilah was

on the girl's heels before anybody could really do anything else. Her boss had said she was the best faker he had ever seen. Yeah, she could fake her way through anything. Most women could. Of course, the "freaking out" came later—

Probably in just a few minutes.

CHAPTER FIVE

S tepping into the hall, Ferrus closed the side wall to the throne room and laughed his ass off. Oh, Mother of the Mountain. That female was the feistiest he'd seen since he was a small child. Before his mother died. In fact, the female reminded him a lot of his mother.

A pang hit his heart, tears burning the back of his eyes. He sucked in a deep breath to keep it together. His mom had left them long ago after a strange illness. His father, the king, thought a witch had poisoned her, but he never could prove that or knew which witch was the culprit.

That was when everything began to change. His father became a man he didn't recognize anymore. The loving dad who doted on his wife and two small children turned cold-hearted and uncaring. His heart had changed to stone as hard and enduring at the mountain they lived in.

No longer were mates allowed together, with the threat of death if caught. Males would train with males and learn to fight, and the females did their duties serving the males and having children. Though Ferrus didn't wholly understand his father's decrees, he was powerless to change them. Until the time he became king, he was to carry out the directives.

But he had found his mate. If he let on who she was, then his father would give orders for her to be killed. What was the big deal about a mate? Yes, she was absolutely stunning, with a body he would enjoy very much, but what else was there? He was a warrior, and she could not protect the clan if she had to. She depended on him to keep her alive.

Oh, Mother of the Mountain, she was *his mate* and as brave as a dragon spewing fire from its mouth. Fitting. They had been born for each other.

No female had spoken to the old king in two hundred sun peaks. The dictate disallowing communicating between the genders, Ferrus thought, was inefficient and unpractical. What did it hurt for a female to talk with a male when needed?

How would she deal with him as her mate? He did not have to tell her, but he had a feeling she already knew, based on the look they shared earlier in the main cavern. She was not of a fae race he was familiar with. He had never smelled anything like her. Was her clan powerful? She said, "where she comes from." He would have to find out where that was. The females in her clan and his could not be more different. She had a lot to learn and adjust to.

They would have to keep their relationship secret like the others did. He did not think he would want to spend much time with her once his animal had his taste of her and could move on. He needed to find a way to be with her at night without raising suspicions. Maybe it was time for him to have a personal female attend to him.

"Ferrus!"

His father's voice carried through the throne room stone wall into the hall leading to his own royal rooms. The man was irritated, all right. He wiped the smile from his face, opened the wall, and stepped into the room.

"You called Father." He coughed to cover a partial laugh that escaped.

"Do not act clueless," his father said. "I saw you standing in the shadows just as your sister was." He stood from his throne. "What do you know of these females? That one will not be alive long if she disobeys the laws again."

Ferrus's dragon roared in his head, making him cringe just a bit. He would not allow that to happen.

His father rubbed his eyes. "I was told there were four transgressors. The other two are the gnoleon spies?"

"Not according to my men. They were hiding from someone farther down the mountainside."

"I find it very convenient that two of the enemy are caught on our land a few cycles before we are to attack."

Ferrus had to agree with his father. But he believed in his guards' abilities. He had trained them, after all.

"I will speak with them," Ferrus said. "Having their group separated makes them weak. We can threaten each with the others' lives if need be. What are you going to do with those two females?" He was almost afraid to hear the answer. He was sure his little mate would not be happy with anything but being released.

And that was not happening whether he wanted her or not. She was never leaving unless it was with him. His men depended on him, so he was not going anywhere.

"They will remain with the rest of the women and do as they are told." His father shrugged like the answer was obvious. The old fool trusted that the foreign women would bend to their rules. One thing he had learned from this meeting, the females—his female—would not go quietly. He worried his father had just stirred the stinger hive. He had a very bad feeling.

Ferrus bowed and backed toward the exiting wall. "I shall make sure the visitors and prisoners are taken care of, Father. Don't worry yourself with them."

"Good, I do not want to hear her voice again. Check with your sister. If they make trouble, return them to the cell, and I will decide what to do with them then."

Chills ran down his back. His father did not mean to decide as in giving them freedom but giving them death.

While Ferra had the other two, he would go to

the holding room to find out what he could from their enemy. Any information about the gnoleon's plans would help with troop formation and time of the attack.

The thought of "attacking" his mate with his tongue buried deep inside her as she screamed his name made him instantly hard. Midstride, he stopped and shook his leg to readjust to an easier walking position. Dragon balls, he had not had this issue in eons. He wondered if the other males had the same problem.

A bit of anger crawled in him from how the mate laws forbade him from doing what he desired. Being the prince, he always got what he wanted. Not that he ever wanted much. He was content in the mountain with his people.

Coming into the restraining room, he nodded to the guard then saw the two gnoleons against the wall. The male was still unconscious. By the female's expression and her care for him, Ferrus figured they were mates. Seeing them together, his heart did a funny thing, stopping him in his tracks.

Here, males and females did not intermingle or touch unless in the sleep room to relieve the males' needs and create children. He wanted to feel his female's body against him. Her lush ass and thighs were perfect for him to kiss and lick and… He stepped back into the tunnel for a moment to get himself under control. How this female made him crazy!

His garment loosening, he re-entered the room to see the female standing at the bars, scowling.

"Where are my friends? What have you done with them?"

He could not help the smile creeping across his face. This one had spirit also. He felt a bond with the male gnoleon concerning bold women.

"Your friends are safe. They are with the other females."

Her eyes narrowed. "What do you want? We mean no harm. We were only crossing over the mountain."

"As I remember," he said, "the cave you were in is not on the trail to the other side."

"We were hiding and planning to be gone as soon as the kappy went away."

His brows arched toward the top of his head. "Kappies? You were hiding from kappies?" He grabbed hold of the bar to keep his balance while he guffawed harder than outside of his father's throne room.

He wiped tears from his eyes. "You were hiding

from kappies? What the mountain for? You cannot be afraid of such little creatures."

"These little creatures burned down an entire forest—"

Ferrus put his hand up, stopping the woman from continuing. Several cycles back, the sky had been filled with opaque smoke that roiled with dark magic. Was that from the burning forest?

The use of the dark powers worried him. That side of the planet's makeup hadn't been strong for a millennium. Many species had fought hard and sacrificed much to live in the peace that now reigned. If the darkness had any chance of returning, they would squash it immediately.

Did any of these four have control of the dark side of the realm? He studied both in the cell, not seeing the shadows around them. Only a few of the more powerful could see the dark magic's presence. He did not get a good enough look at his mate and the female with her. He needed more light.

Turning, he left the room quickly. "I shall return." He needed to find out if his mate wielded any abilities that would get her killed.

CHAPTER SIX

Ascending a very long twisty tunnel, Lilah followed the young lady who she supposed was the king's daughter—a female who couldn't speak to the king. How idiotic could someone be? Women not talking to men? She couldn't imagine the sexual frustration this place must be full of. Men *and* women.

If anyone knew about sexual frustration, it was her. She hadn't dated since her senior year in college five years ago. Her battery-powered boyfriend had been her best friend. He had never body-shamed her, told her she was too fat to fuck, or she should eat more salads. No, he appreciated the fact that she kept his batteries full and running. That would've been the only male who valued her.

Maybe this separation of the sexes was a great idea. The women wouldn't have to put up with men's stupid shit, and the men didn't have to put up with women trying to make them better.

Wiping sweat from her forehead, legs becoming wobbly, Lilah wondered where they were going and how much longer it would take. When leaving the throne room, she didn't think to ask. She wanted away from that old fart so badly. This girl did not look threatening, so Lilah had no problem going with her.

Now that she'd had time to think, she needed to pull her shit together. They needed to get Wren and Zee out of the prison cell and get the hell out of this place.

"Excuse me, Ferra?" She thought that was the girl's name. The daughter turned back to her. "We need to get our friends and get back on the road. Can you help us with that?"

The young lady's head tilted, brows drawn down. "You are one of us now. You do not need to go anywhere."

Lilah chuckled and put an arm around the girl's shoulders, the dumb cover-up limiting her movements. "You do not understand, honey. This is not our home. We are trying to get back to our family.

You wouldn't want someone to keep you from being here with your dad, right?"

Ferra shook her head then twisted around, maneuvering Lilah's hand into hers. "Come meet the others." The girl reached out to Daphne, who took the offering.

"We can stay for a little bit. How's that?" Daphne glanced at her over the head between them. Her cousin's comment was a good idea. They needed time to come up with a plan to escape anyway. She gave a nod to Daph, and the girl led them up the tunnel, and up, and up.

By the time they came to where light penetrated the dark passage, her legs were jelly. They'd been dragging Daph the last mile or so. Geesh. Had they climbed to the top of the damn mountain?

They entered a room that had her jaw dropping. She glanced at her cousin. Daph's eyes were as wide as donuts, which sounded good at the moment since they had berries and grains for breakfast a few hours ago.

The space they entered was huge, with sunlight pouring in. Lilah's eyes needed a minute to adjust to the brightness. Ferra dropped their hands and rushed forward toward other ladies. Some with brown sheets on, some with them off.

The females' clothing was very different from the gnoleon's. Where the tree people wore animal hide and bead necklaces to cover their flat chests, these women had a smaller version of the ghost sheets but with no head covering. It looked like they wore a T-shirt that was two sizes too big.

But the most important thing she noted was that they all had big thighs and butts. With all the climbing they had to do, having larger muscles in that area of the body made perfect sense.

Lilah slipped her coverall over her head and laid it over her arm. Daph just pushed the hood back. As the two stood at the entrance, the women started noticing them. Many women stood along a rectangular island in the middle of the cavern, like many kitchens on earth had. They held small knives, and stone bowls of food were scattered about. Smelled like food, anyway.

On the far side, women came down a slope, carrying larger bowls filled with stuff, stopping when seeing her and her cousin. An elder set her blade on the stone island and approached them.

"Welcome," she greeted, "I am Valori." She bowed her head slightly.

Daphne made the same move. "Thank you for the welcome. I am Daphne, and this is Lilah."

Ferra rushed toward them, chewing on something like a carrot. "Valori, Father said for them to learn our ways."

Valori jerked around. "Why? They are not one of us."

The girl shrugged.

Lilah smiled, coming out of her stupor. "We are not staying long. In fact, we should be leaving now." She pivoted on the ball of her foot and walked back the way they came. Daphne caught up to her.

"Do you know how to get us out of here?" her cousin whispered.

Lilah stopped. Of course, she didn't. Dammit. She stared down the dark slope they had climbed. Shit. "What do we do, Daph?" she asked. Her usual bravado and confidence were gone in the face of failing her friends and thoughts of never getting home.

Her cousin turned back to the women. "Since we just got here, we'd love to have a tour of the place."

Oh my god. Daph was a genius. She would've never thought of something so brilliant. Though she had to admit, she didn't give Daphne much credit when it came to anything.

When they were young, Lilah's mom always belittled her by saying things like, *why can't you be skinnier like your cousin,* and *why don't you try to be smarter like Daphne.* After a while, young Lilah came to dislike her friend as Lilah's mom continued to compare the two, Lilah always being the one lacking.

For years, Lilah had dreamed of running away so Daphne could take her place in the family. Maybe then her mom would've been happy not stuck with such a disappointment as Lilah.

As they grew older, her mother had stopped her ugly words, but the damage was done. To Lilah's mind, brushing off Daphne made her cousin a flawed person. If Daphne wasn't perfect, maybe one day, Lilah's mother would appreciate Lilah for who she was.

Now, as an adult, Lilah tried not to remember those times as a child, but the hurt and feelings of being a failure to her mother still cut deeply.

The worst part about it all was that Daphne had no idea how much resentment had built up during the younger years. And through no fault of her cousin's own. The girl was innocent of everything but being herself.

Maybe it was time to let all that go. Daphne

really was a smart woman, even if she was willowy and tall and graceful and all the things Lilah wanted to be. She had accepted that her body was what it was and worked to keep herself as healthy as possible.

But she also had the philosophy that if she was going to be alive, she wasn't going to hate every moment by eating bland, tasteless food. If she was to live, it would be on her terms, and she was enjoying a big juicy, buttery, steak when she wanted. What was the point of living if you wished you didn't?

"Oh, Elder Val," a woman on the slope covered in sunshine called out, "I will take them on a tour of our home."

Turning to Lilah and Daph, the elder rolled her eyes. "Shinni would love to show you the improved garden. And, of course, the rest of our mountain if there is time."

The woman almost skipped across the floor to them. "Come. Let me show you what we've done."

Lilah looked at Daphne, who shrugged. If they wanted to find the way out, they'd have to take the scenic route. The two followed Shinni up the slope, and to Lilah's surprise, out into the open air. Quite chilly air. Looking around, she realized why it was cold. The clouds couldn't have been more than a hundred feet above them. And the ground was at least *three* hundred feet below.

Instinctually, she jerked backward from the edge and into Daphne. Her friend wrapped an arm around her. "I got you, Lil. I won't let anything hurt you."

Those words melted into her heart. She looked over her shoulder to see Daphne's serious expression. Her friend meant those words. A little bit of the hurt she'd involuntarily harbored against her cousin vanished.

"Over here," Shinni said, waving them to cross onto a sizeable flattened area of dirt with crops. Damn, they did have a garden—on a mountain top. Who would've thought?

Not only were the crops growing, but they also looked like a large dose of Miracle Grow had been used. How did they even carry a melon the size of a beach ball? Shinni gabbed on about the food items, much of which meant little to Lilah since she had never tasted any of them. They looked unlike the gnoleon melons and root food items.

The dirt even looked different. She squatted and grabbed a handful. The texture was strange. The color was a mix of grey and brown.

"And that's what I discovered," Shinni said, crouching next to Lilah. "By adding ash from the volcano to the dirt brought up from the forest, everything has almost doubled in size. It's fantastic." The woman's eyes shined along with her smile.

Wait a minute. There was a word in that last bit of what the sunburned fae had said that surprised her.

"Shinni, hold on. Did you say 'volcano'?"

The fae tilted her head like Ferra had done earlier. "Of course, where do you think the metal for the swords and knives come from?"

Honestly, she hadn't thought about it. The forest dwellers didn't have metal utensils. They ate with wooden sticks like chopsticks. When they arrived in the main cave, the soldiers were training with large, heavy metal weapons.

"What does a volcano have to do with metal?" Daphne asked. That was Lilah's next question also.

"The magma has the metal in a liquid form. The smith takes out the liquid and shapes it into forms we need. Most is used for weapons. The swords break so much that we need a constant supply for the soldiers to keep training." Shinni scowled then rose and walked away, mumbling, "If the males would listen to us, then they wouldn't have so many problems."

What did that mean? Daphne glanced at her as she must've heard it too. All righty then. Lilah stood, dropping the soil.

"Let's go inside, and I'll show you around the food preparation area." The fae gracefully floated over the rugged terrain to the slope like a prima ballerina. Lilah was as far from that as could be. Daphne grabbed her hand and pulled her along, helping her keep her balance on the tilted mountainside between the garden and kitchen entrance.

Stepping onto the slope, she noticed a mirror inserted into the rock wall. "What's that for?" she asked. Then she saw how the light bounced off it, going farther into the cave. Her eyes followed the invisible trail to another two reflectors.

Good god. She hadn't thought about it when they had first arrived in the kitchen, but the space was brightly lit. Not a torch to be seen. Not that using mirrors to move light was a new concept, but making it really work was impressive. Couldn't they bounce light down to the main cavern? Was it too far down?

Shinni took them away from the stone island toward another space where she heard water running. Women not in brown ponchos stood over a raised basin with a small waterfall coming through a hole in the ceiling. The sight was charming, with sunlight shining off the water—the perfect place to have a picnic if they hadn't been in a mountain.

Seeing one of the women stepping away with a dripping load in her arms, she realized they were washing clothes. The fae moved into an area with row after row of thin rock walls about four feet tall. Clothes of all sizes were draped over the tops —even children's garments.

Many girls of all ages roamed the kitchen area, helping the women. But where were the boys? Were they with the soldiers? That was a bit old fashioned if you asked her. Some of the best chefs were men. And she knew some women who could totally beat any man's ass in a mixed martial arts cage.

Coming back to the island where women cut and diced food, Lilah noted the women who had their brown sheets off had bodies the same shape as she did. The climb from the throne room to here solidified in her mind the reason for such muscle-laden bottoms.

Not paying attention to her surroundings, her

elbow bumped a bowl off the surface to break into stone pieces when it hit the floor. Horror shot through Lilah. How long did it take them to carve the large bowls from rock? Days? Weeks?

"Don't worry," the woman next to her said, bending over to gather the pieces. The fae set the chunks on the island and mashed the parts in her hands like they were dough. As Lilah and Daphne watched, the female squashed the doughy sections into one gray ball then worked it into a bowl shape. She moved the dish to the middle of the table, where it slowly hardened into the rock it had been.

Holy shisterbots! That was amazing. Their magic was manipulating the material they had in abundance—stone. That explained the stone cups, plates, and other items lying around. Her attention went to the knives used to cut food.

The blades were shiny and looked sharp as hell as they sliced through carrot-looking items with ease. The swords which the warriors trained with didn't shine. She wondered if there was a difference between the two materials that made each.

"Shinni," Lilah said, "do you have the same problem with your knives as the guys do with their swords breaking?" The raucous reaction from the women startled her. Some slammed their knives on the table. Some gave her a look of disgust. Others snorted. "What?" Lilah asked, afraid she'd said something to offend them.

The woman standing beside her stopped chopping. "The men do as they wish. If they want to be stupid and not listen to us, then that's their loss."

"What do you mean?" Daphne asked. Valori gave the woman a sharp glance, and she returned to her work.

"It is of no matter," the elder said then nodded her head toward her and Daph. "Give Lilah a chunk of rock."

Daph leaned over Lilah's shoulder. "Why are they doing that?" Lilah shrugged, as a fae went to a wall with several pockmarks. Her fingers sank into the hard stone like it was sand, and she scooped out a large handful. Lilah followed the fae's movement toward her, and the small boulder the dainty hands set on the table in front of her.

Lilah looked up at the others. No one paid her any attention. What was she supposed to do with this?

Valori glanced at her. "Go on. Make you and your friend a cup to drink from."

"What?" Lilah replied. "How?"

Valori responded with a scowl. "Split the rock in half." Lilah lifted the rock and banged it against the tabletop. Giggles went around the work area.

Why did the old woman think she could mold the rock like they could? That was ridiculous. Despite the stupidity, she mimicked what the other woman did to dig the rock from the wall. She placed her fingers over the center of the stone and slowly pushed them down. The hard surface pressing against her tips gave, and she slid her hand through, splitting the rock.

Daphne's jaw dropped, and she snatched half of the rock and pounded her fingers against it, unsuccessfully. Lilah dug her thumbs into the clay-like material and hollowed out the center like she'd done as a kid with colorful sculpting clay. The soft material warmed even more against her palm, bending and stretching as her fingers demanded.

"How are you doing that?" her cousin whispered. She just shrugged. "Here." Lilah took the other stone half and repeated to make another cup. After finishing the second dish, the first had transformed back into hard rock.

"Now, you can get your own water to drink." Elder Valori nodded to the side where tall barrel-like containers sat. She and Daphne approached them, seeing water in each. She dipped her cup into the liquid then drank water tasting better than the day before in the forest.

"Bring two chunks of rock back with you," the elder said.

Lilah handed her cup to Daph and dug out two handfuls of the closest wall. "Very good," Valori said, "but we have a special a wall to take from. You can't be all willy-nilly where you take from the wall strength."

Lilah panicked, thinking the ceiling would cave in on top of them, and slapped the material back into place. Her hands sunk in up to her wrists. The ladies giggled again. Her face heated as she yanked her arms free.

Daphne led her to the place the other lady had claimed their cups. "Here," she said. Lilah scooped out a couple holes, and they returned to the stone island prep area. Her head was in a tailspin. How was she able to do this? Nothing like this happened on earth. Though she never tried to make a mug from a rock.

"You know," Daphne said, voice low, "Wren can make tree limbs bend to make chairs. Maybe you can bend rocks to make dishes."

"Like that's helpful." Lilah rolled her eyes.

Daph shrugged. "I can't do it."

"Now," Valori said from the other side of the work island, "crush one of those into dust." One of the females looked up with surprise, noticing no one else reacting, then went back to chopping.

Lilah did as instructed and squeezed a chunk in her hand, picturing in her mind's eye the stone breaking into pieces and turning to dust. As she gripped, the hard resistance gave, and the rock disintegrated in her hand.

"Cool," Daphne replied to Lilah's accomplishment.

Valori nodded to the other piece of stone. "Change that into a solid piece of metal." This time, all the women stopped and stared at the elder. Valori's eyes never wavered from hers. Heads swiveled in her direction. Why were the ladies freaking out?

Having no idea how to transform rock to metal, she picked up the second chunk. Just like she had with the previous slab, she imagined what she wanted to happen. The room was so silent, she heard water trickling somewhere in the distance. The happy, smiling faces were frozen with gaping jaws and bugged-out eyes.

Her heart pounded against her chest hard

enough to almost hurt. She didn't know how long this process would take if she could do it. She felt a vibration under her feet just before a rumbling of voices reached her. That snapped everyone from their stupor in an instant, and controlled chaos broke out.

Women rushed around, grabbing bowls and dishes and jugs. Someone scooted a bowl across the stone toward her. She released the rock to see it was the same color as the men's swords, then grabbed the bowl.

"Wait," Farra handed the brown sheet to her, "you must put this on."

"I don't need it," Lilah replied. "I'm not cold anymore."

"No," the young lady said, "you *have* to wear it."

Lilah propped a hand on her hip. "Why do I *have* to wear it if I don't want to?"

Valori appeared at her side, taking the cover-up and slipping it over Lilah's head. "Because it is safer for females to have it on."

That made no sense. "How does this flimsy material protect me from anything except a cool breeze?"

The elder's red-tinted face darkened along her cheeks. "If the males see any skin of a female, except their face, they might not be able to control themselves." The voices became louder and clearer. It sounded like a large herd of elephants were nearby.

Lilah waited for the rest of the explanation as she slipped her arms through the garment's holes. When she didn't get it, she asked. "Control themselves how?"

The woman shoved the bowl of sliced potato-like food into her hands. Daphne had disappeared. "Come with me," Valori directed. They left the room, stepping into a hallway with a score of other women dashing in and out of an archway at the other end.

Then the purpose of a cover-up rang in her head. "Do men hit women or abuse them?" Instant fury ignited in her stomach.

"No," Valori's demeanor turned defensive, "of course not. Touching is not allowed. For the most part." Lilah drew her brows down, not understanding what the woman was trying to say. "Control themselves from becoming overly excited by the sight of flesh."

The meaning clicked. "Wait," Lilah came to an abrupt stop in the middle of the passage, "are you saying that because the men can't keep it in their pants, *we* are subjected to wearing this even when we don't want to?" Each word got higher in pitch 'till she was nearly screeching. "You have got to be fucking kidding me."

Valori shushed her and dragged her through the arch into a large cavern with stone tables and chairs. Dishes and bowls of food sat on the tables, the others filling each stone plate and cup. Oh, they were eating. She was getting a bit hungry as breakfast was a while ago. The elder took the container from her and put it on a table. "Not now. Be quiet."

Valori pulled her against the wall as the soldiers came in and took seats. The tables filled quickly. She wondered where the women were going to sit. Slowly, it dawned on her.

The women weren't supposed to sit. They were there to serve. Oh, fuck no! This was not happening. She was an American and would not stand for shit like this.

CHAPTER SEVEN

Ferrus hurried from the dungeon to the main cavern. Not seeing the woman he desired, he headed toward his sister's room. Hopefully, they were there. If not, he would have to go up to the food area. He had not been there since he was a child.

He followed the tunnel to the royal rooms, to find them deserted. Irritated, he started the climb to the top of the mountain. Ferrus imagined seeing his mate again, taking her into his arms and feeling her skin against his.

As he reached the upper levels, he noticed the tunnel had more light than those below. How was that happening?

The floor vibrated, and it sounded like a herd

of hornbill was bolting up the tunnels. What the demon's hell? In the hall between the food prep and eating cave, females dashed back and forth. The light was so bright that he stayed around the corner of the passage. That is when he heard her voice. And it did not sound pleased.

Not only was the sound unhappy, but it was also angry. He wanted to know what made her that way and crush it. Nothing in this world would upset her. He would keep her safe and happy.

When he heard his soldier's voices, he realized what the hornbill herd was. Dragon balls! Did they always sound like that? The females moving from the prep room to the eatery had stopped. He hurried along the aisle, shielding his eyes, to the darker tunnel the males emerged from and followed them into the room.

Searching the space, he saw her on the far side with one of the elders beside her. Dragon dung! The fire in her eyes set him ablaze. She was so sexy with the red tint on her cheeks. He sat at his place at one of the many square tables and tried not to stare. But his eyes kept migrating to her beauty.

He wanted to see her again without the cover-up. But that would have to wait until tonight. No fae would lay his eyes or hands on her and live.

When he peeked up at her again, she was staring at him. He couldn't move his eyes from hers. When the corners of her mouth turned up, his heart flipped in his chest. Was that normal? He'd been experiencing such strange things since she walked in. Could she have been a witch and put a spell on him?

His mate—what was her name? Lilah?—lifted a water jug and walked around the room toward him. Was she coming to see him? His dragon wanted out to taste her, but despite being in the eating room, there would be no eating of their mate right now. Though the thought made his dick hard. Thank the Mother of the Mountain, they were seated at a table.

She floated to his side and held up the jug. He lifted his cup and turned in his chair, so they faced away from his men. This would be an excellent time to see if she had dark magic clinging to her.

He narrowed his eyes and spoke first. "I saw you earlier." He didn't see any shadows around her hands or head.

She poured water into his cup. "I am not supposed to talk with men, right?"

"I disagree with that law. How are we to get things done if I cannot tell you what I want." Her brow raised and lips puckered. How he wanted to kiss them.

"What you want?" she whispered. "Of course." She bowed. "I am your humble servant, master." Her actions surprised him. He didn't think she knew he was the prince. He did not want her to know yet. He wanted her real reaction to him, not his place in the hierarchy.

He replied. "I am just a humble warrior here among the males." He flashed her his best smile. Her eyes dropped to his mouth, and she licked her lips. He barely suppressed the groan that escaped his throat—Goddess, how he wanted to touch her.

"Since you are with the females, do you plan on staying? Apparently, the king isn't worried about you leaving."

She snorted. "This place is a damn maze. The king knows we couldn't get out if we tried."

"That was the plan when our home here was created."

Her brows raised again. "To ensnare women?"

He frowned. "No, to keep the enemy out or intruders from getting away." He glanced at the men at his table who had their heads down eating, unlike others in the room who talked and laughed. "Perhaps later, we can meet and"—*strip our clothes off and have sex until we can't see straight*—"exchange information about our different cultures."

He knew what he was asking was against the established rules, but he couldn't help it. Lilah's eyes narrowed at him. "Why are you being so nice to me? Your king was a chauvinistic asshat to us."

Part of her last sentence didn't make sense to him. He had never heard the words *chauvinistic asshat*, but they did not sound praising coming from her.

"The king is set in his ways. Many of us think differently."

"Does the king know that? Y'all might get your heads chopped off."

Her nonchalance about such a gruesome act had him taken aback. There had been those in the past who had done something horrific and were punished as so. Was her culture so cruel that such things were commonplace? No wonder she was so strong in her words and actions. She was a survivor. His regard for her rose.

A disturbance at the back of the room drew his attention. It seemed Silvo was causing problems again. If the man hadn't been such a good warrior, he would have sent Silvo to the town to work security for someone.

"Who is that?" she asked. "I don't like him by his looks alone. His attitude is similar to the kings. Is that his son by chance?"

Ferrus chuckled, keeping an eye on his second-in-command. "He certainly fits the part."

The soldier stood and yelled at a female holding a water jug.

"Why did you spill water on me?" When the female didn't answer, he yelled, "Answer me."

"I-I am—" Before she could get any more words out, he backhanded her, knocking her to the floor.

"Females are not allowed to talk to males. You should be thrown in the dungeon."

Lilah set the water jug on the table with a thump. "Oh, fuck, no. That ain't flying with me."

Before Ferrus could reprimand the female server, his mate was swinging into action.

"Hey, douchebag!" she shouted at Silvo while she stomped toward the female on the floor, "that's entrapment, and no jury would convict her. You, on the other hand, are guilty of assault and battery. I can put your ass in jail for a year."

The warrior's face turned redder. "You are not to speak to me. I am—"

"An idiot. Thanks for letting everyone else know too." While his mate helped up the female,

Ferrus carefully watched his warrior. If the soldier made any threatening move toward his mate, he would take the man's balls personally. Even though the laws were against her, Ferrus didn't care.

Little Lilah picked up the container of water the other female had and snatched Silvo's cup from the table. Not taking her eyes from him, she filled it then slammed it on the table, saying, "The next time you create a scene to have a reason to be an ass, pick on someone your own size. Hopefully, they will do to you what you did to her." She set the water jug on the table next to him. "If you want any more, pour it yourself."

Silvo opened his mouth, but his mate had spun on her heel and was walking out. "Daphne," she said, looking around, "let's get the hell out of here. I've had enough of this male domination BS. We got important shit to do." The other female who arrived with her ran after her.

The room erupted into murmurs as they stomped into the hallway. Dragon balls! What was he supposed to do? He didn't care what the rules were dictating a situation as odd as this. He was not letting her out of his sight. He would not let her walk out of his life even if he couldn't have her.

He left the room, trailing them from a

distance. They passed the food prep room and continued down the long tunnel toward the cavern. The entire time his female went on and on about men and one thing or another. He had no idea there were so many things wrong with their gender.

"Lilah," her friend asked, "do you know where you're going?"

"We went straight to the kitchen from the king's room. So, we just go past there, and the big middle section should be nearby. From there, we can get to Wren and Zee and get the fuck out of this fresh hell."

When the two turned the wrong way for the main cavern, he wondered if he should stop them. The tunnel they took led down to the mines. He needed to speak with the smith about stronger swords, so he might as well take care of that now. Yes, his dragon liked that idea. Maybe Ferrus could impress her with how strong and well-armed they were as an army. He would be able to always keep her safe.

He stayed back from the two, but his dragon's hearing picked up their conversation. Daphne had asked why she was so angry. His mate told her how the females were forced to wear something called "sheets" due to the men not being able to "keep it in their pants."

He glanced down at his clothing, which consisted of close-fitting bottoms that kept the delicate items safely tucked up. Other than that, there wasn't much to get in the way of training and fighting. His body was mostly exposed, which the women were not allowed to do.

Seeing it in that perspective, it didn't seem right that females *had* to cover themselves and the men did not. When he was very young, he remembered the women wearing different clothing that showed their arms and legs. He couldn't remember exactly when that changed.

The air became heavier with dust particles. They were getting closer to the mines. He had almost caught up with the females and needed to slow down.

Suddenly, the girls faced him as if deciding to walk back up. They both screamed when seeing him. He threw his hands up in front of him. "Sorry, females," he said.

His mate's eyes widened as she stared at him.

The other female asked, "Were you following us? Who are you?"

He couldn't help the smirk on his lips at the

beautiful female's fixation on him. Yes, she was affected by him as he was by her.

"I am going to the smith's cave to speak with him. I do not know where you are going."

Daphne continued to speak since Lilah said nothing. "We made a wrong turn somewhere and are going back."

"I would be more than glad to escort you to where you want to go." His eyes never left his mate's.

"Oh," the tall female looked at his mate still staring at him. "Uh, we don't want to keep you from whatever you're doing."

He smiled his best smile and stepped toward Lilah. "You won't be." He gestured with his arm for them to continue down with him, laying his hand on the small of his mate's back. "I will show you the most impressive weapons cave you have ever seen."

Tingles raced through his body on contact with her. He couldn't tell her reaction since it was hidden by the extra clothing. He wanted so much to touch her skin, feel its softness, silkiness. Maybe they could find a corner where they could "meet" each other.

He'd been blabbing the whole walk down to the

mine and really had no idea what he said. His mind was so involved in both her and her reactions to him. When they reached the dig area, his mate was sweating. He had forgotten how hot it was in the volcano's depths.

"Smits," Ferrus called out. He watched as his mate studied the young boys carrying in rock from the mine and the magma female drenched in sweat at the lava river. His mate's wide eyes and gaping mouth probably weren't a good thing.

Great. Now, what was wrong?

CHAPTER EIGHT

Lilah was so pissed when she walked out of the dining room, she could've chewed the entire rock wall and spit it out like bullets from a machine gun. All at one man, well two: that asshole who liked to hurt women and the dumbass king for his stupider than dog shit laws.

That one nice man, though, she had seen him when she walked in. She'd wished that the light hadn't been so dim in the room. She couldn't see much more than his silhouette as he sat. She would have loved to see what all of him looked like up close. That would be a wet dream come true. But right now, she had more important things to think about.

It was time to get the hell out of this place. If the guards tried to stop them, she'd deal with it then. Right now she was too angry. Reaching the kitchen entrance, she made sure her cousin was with her then continued down the slope toward the king's throne room where this whole nightmare began.

Could she tell off the bastard and not be thrown back in their cell? Probably not. Maybe she could try to be such a pain in the ass that His Hind Ass would tell them to leave. She doubted that too. Judges didn't release the attorneys for bad behavior; they called contempt of court. And sitting in jail while the judge cooled his jets wasn't fun. She learned that the second time she had to sit and wait.

"Lilah," her friend asked, "do you know where you're going?"

"We went straight to the kitchen from the king's room. So, we just go past that, and the big cavern should be nearby. From there, we can get to Wren and Zee and get the fuck out of this fresh hell."

"Lilah," Daph whispered, getting closer to her, "why are you ready to chew someone a new hole?

Granted, that guy back there who hit the woman deserves to have his left nut cut off, but you've been like this since we left the village this morning."

Lilah squeezed her hands into fists, letting the bite of her nails into her palm help her to get a grip on herself. There was no way she would tell Daphne about her jealousy of Wren finding a mate, the loneliness she had endured for so long, and the humiliation she suffered daily from others because of her weight.

"I am guessing you didn't hear me in the hall before I got to the dining room where women work for free and get shitty tips."

Daph shook her head. "No, someone shoved a bowl in my hands and told me to follow them while the older lady helped you put on your poncho."

"Let me tell you about this lovely prison garment." She tugged on the covering and went on to tell her cousin what Valori had told her about the men subjugating the women because they couldn't keep it in their pants.

"That's a bunch of bull hockey," Daph replied.

She snorted. "Not quite what I said, but yeah.

Then there were women serving the men and not eating themselves. Then to top it off, that bully showed no respect for what the women were doing for the men. Not to mention that women aren't allowed to talk to men because of gender."

Daphne laughed as they passed the throne room door. "I knew that would piss you off." When they came to an intersection, Lilah guided them to the right. Daphne said, "I remember that case a couple years back when a woman who was a welder sued for discrimination. You were so awesome with the jury. I don't see why you aren't a partner at the office yet. The men there are idiots."

Discrimination based on sex happened at more than blue-collar jobs. But she loved what she did, so she hadn't complained since it was just her affected. The thing was she couldn't stand to see an injustice. When someone was wronged, her inner demon flared to life, wanting revenge on the wrongdoer, to make him pay for the harm he'd caused.

She couldn't beat the shit out of those people, so she took them to court.

"I've had enough of this place to last me forever," she mumbled. "If they want to live in the stone age, then let them. But we are finding a way out if I have to crush every piece of rock to do it."

"I forgot about that. How did you do that?"

She shrugged. "It just happened. I have no clue." Lilah wiped her forehead. "It's getting hot."

"I noticed. I don't think we're in the right tunnel. We've been walking too long."

She scowled. "I think you're right. We probably should've turned left instead of right." When she pivoted on the ball of her foot, movement caught the edge of her eye, and she screamed from being startled. Daphne did the same. And holy shit.

It was him. This was the first time she had seen him up close and…all of him. Their training "uniform" of short-shorts type of covering outlined everything it hid. All she could do was stare at his perfection. Everything about him was fine, head to toe.

Yeah, so she understood how men could get riled up at seeing a woman scantily clad, but was she about to attack the man? No. Not because she didn't want to, but because she had control over herself. Enough for the moment anyway. If she could keep it in her pants, so could the men here.

Her eyes fixed on his plump lips as he spoke.

His voice was sweet music in her head. She breathed him in. He smelled like crisp, clean air like after a snowfall. Next thing she knew, he had his hand on her back, guiding her farther down the tunnel. Where were they going? She didn't care as long as he was with her.

Then she saw boys coming out of a hole, coughing from the dust-laden air, carrying containers of crushed rock to dump into a huge cauldron. At the black pot, a young woman as wet as a fish worked a device that lowered the large kettle to the top of a lava flow. Wait, she wasn't doused in water, but sweat. And the kids were mine laborers.

She stared back and forth between the two areas. She didn't know which was worse. Which was the most significant, most unethical treatment on the planet?

Wanting to know what was going on, she went to the woman manning the cauldron.

"Don't you have any water? When was your last break? Are you the only one doing this?"

The lady's eyes widened, and she stepped back, closer to the edge leading into the lava.

"Stop!" Lilah said, holding her hands out. She slowly pointed. "Don't fall in." The woman glanced into the pot hovering just above the molten rock river. With a long hook, she rolled it toward her and to the side where stone molds in the shape of swords lay. She tipped the pot, and liquid poured into each mold. To the side were stacks of swords ready to go.

"This is how you make your weapons?" she asked the lady who just squinted at her. Then Lilah watched as the woman picked up a boulder the size of two softballs and shaped it into a hilt, then inserted it in a notch at the end of the cast. Viola, a sword.

Lilah asked, "Why are you making so many?" The woman covered her lips. Lilah didn't understand. "What? You're not allowed to talk about it?" The lady opened her mouth, pointed inside it, then put her hand over her lips again. "Oh, you can't talk at all?" Sad eyes met hers.

A while back, she worked with a hearing-impaired client from whom she learned to sign the alphabet. God, did she still remember all that? Wait. She shook her head. She had forgotten where she was. Sign language in a foreign dimension probably wouldn't work. Then a thought hit her.

"Blink once for yes, twice for no. Are you

working down here because you aren't able to talk to others?"

The lady's eyes widened and blinked once.

"Would you rather be in the kitchen than down here?"

The sad eyes returned, but they glanced toward the other side where the small boys were bringing out more dust.

Well, she'd wondered where the boys were. She got her answer. Which, of course, pissed her off even more. Their lungs must've been damaged to the point of breathing problems. Why didn't these people see this? Hello? Mesothelioma, lung cancer, anyone?

Just more inequalities and discrimination to put on the growing list. Taking off her brown sheet, she wiped her face and went back to where Daph stood with Mr. Sexy and some other man. Both guys' eyes were wide. What? Had they never seen a woman before? The older man with shock and her guy (where had *her* come from?), were checking her out, head to toe. She didn't even want to know what he thought about her body.

She'd heard it plenty of times in the past. *You're pretty but too big. Your ass is too fat for me. Can't you go to the gym?* Instead, she asked the question she had for the woman. "Why are you making so many swords? There aren't this many men here, are there?"

The older man had his mouth hanging open still, so she looked to Hotstuff. "We're going to war," he said.

Lilah rolled her eyes. "Fabulous, let me guess. You want someone else's land, so instead of negotiating, you kill others."

The elder man gasped. "You can't speak to the prin—"

"It's fine, Smit. I have given her special permission," he said.

Hell, she didn't even know who her guy was. "What's your name, anyway?"

He made a proper bow to her. "I am Ferrus Ironback, my lady."

She scowled even though butterflies swarmed in her stomach. "You're breaking about every child labor law that exists, you know that, right?"

Ferrus drew his brows down. "We have no child labor rules."

"Of course not," she said. "There is no one here to stand up to the powers that would exploit them. Neither do the women for that matter." The thought that she could be that person, that she could be the one to bring justice to these unfairly treated people, intrigued her. First, they needed to get Wren and Zee out of their cell.

"Why are Daphne and I not in the holding tank with the other two? Why can't our friend and her mate come out too?"

Ferrus stared at her for a minute, then turned and started up the slope.

"Hey," Lilah called out, "don't walk away and not answer me. That's rude." She jogged to catch up to his long strides. "Why can't they be released too? In fact, if you release them, we will be on our way, and you'll never see us again."

Ferrus stopped. His eyes held anger. He backed her against the tunnel wall, not touching her, but damn close. "I am never letting you go. Get used to that right now. You are mine." He stared into her eyes, making her breathless and speechless. Wait. Was he hitting on her? Was this his way of asking a woman on a date? Pretty piss poor if it was.

Why would someone as gorgeous as he was want to be with someone like her? She was far from perfect, and he deserved nothing less.

This was a situation she'd never been in. In school, the boys wanted just one thing, and when they became too demanding, she dumped them for someone else. That was the only reason she had a "new boyfriend every week," according to Wren and Daph. If they knew the truth, they would've known how hurt she was by their comment.

He grinned. "Nothing to say for once?"

Bastard. She shoved him away. Her anger rose fast. "I belong to no one. You get used to *that*." She stomped down the tunnel to where Daphne stood, watching the two of them with eyes wide and a huge smile on her face. "What?" she griped when reaching her cousin.

Daph's smile faded. "He just said he wants you. Hello?"

Lilah crossed her arms over her chest. "Well, I don't want him. He's an arrogant ass who is too good-looking." She heard him chuckling from up the tunnel.

"Oh," he said without turning back, "your friends are staying where they are. I will not allow the enemy to roam freely through our home."

Lilah locked eyes with Daph. Lilah asked, "Did he just say, enemy?"

Daphne replied, "He said they're going to war."

"Oh my god," Lilah breathed.

"They are going to kill everyone in Zee's village."

Lilah spun around and ran. "Come on, Daph. We have to stop them."

"How?"

"We're going to talk to the king again."

Hopefully, it would go better this time.

CHAPTER NINE

Lilah and her cousin dashed past a walking Ferrus. They didn't have time to debate with some warrior about not going to war over…

"Hey," Lilah stopped in the middle of the tunnel, "why are you going to fight the gnoleon? What did they do to you?"

His surprised expression stupefied her. He answered, "You came from the village, did you not? Surely you know of their plans to take over the mountain."

Again, she was almost speechless. Almost. "Are you crazy? Why in the world would they give up living in the forest to move into a big-ass hole in the ground where there's no sunshine or fresh air."

"Not to mention," Daphne added, "their magic works on dirt and growing plants. Don't see too much of that here."

He stopped in front of her, feet set shoulder-width apart. "Then tell me why they suddenly show up not far from here?"

"Because their forest burned down." Lilah and Daph said together, then grinned at each other.

He sighed. "That's what the female gnoleon said."

Was he talking about Wren? "Have you spoken to Wren and Zee?"

"Briefly. They said the same thing about their forest. But who would do such a thing? The qhasant have been wiped out for hundreds of years."

Oh shit. They didn't know about the kappy army trying to get their hands on her, Daphne, and Wren for their portal rocks. Her hand slid over her pocket and felt a bump. Still there.

She spun around, hurrying up the tunnel. "We have to speak with the king now. There is something he doesn't know. Something new."

"What?" He moved up to her side.

"Daph," Lilah said, "is your gemstone in your

pocket?" Her cousin slapped fingers over her hip and nodded.

"That is what their leader wants, isn't it? We need to talk to Wren too. She knows more than we do."

Lilah gasped. "Yes, she does." She turned to the hunk beside her. "The two in prison have details about this guy who has an army or something." He stumbled but kept up. "If you want to know it all, then they need to be there too."

His eyes narrowed. "Army? What army?"

"You'll know more when Wren arrives in the throne room. If she doesn't, then you don't get the intel."

He growled. She felt the air vibrate from his chest. The man actually sounded like a wild animal. "Keep walking straight. Don't make any turns, and this will lead to the main cavern. From there, we'll go to the king's room."

With that, he was gone in a blink. Not vanishing into thin air, but moving so quickly, her eyes couldn't track him in the torchlight.

"You got a plan?" Daphne asked, sounding hopeful.

"I'm not sure. First, we need to keep these guys from attacking. Then we need to figure out how to get out of here. If they find out who Zee is, they might kill him and Wren."

Daph gasped. "Shit, he's the alph—"

"Yes, don't say it. Anyone could be listening." They passed the tunnel from the kitchen and continued straight. She knew she should've turned left instead of right. Dammit.

When they reached the cavern, Lilah debated whether she wanted to cause a big scene right now. She was getting tired and hungry. God, this was so stupid.

In the main cavern, Wren and Zee stood waiting. A small army surrounded them. The girls greeted each other with hugs, and Lilah spared a touch for Zee.

When hugging him, she whispered into his ear, "Don't tell them who you are." She pulled away. "Glad to see you're awake now." She caught Ferrus's eyes glowering at her. His hands were around the hilt of his sword strapped to his back. What was his problem?

"Snap to it." She snapped her finger at the red fae. "To the throne room." Was it her imagination, or did the big guy's face become redder? She smiled to herself. He deserved that just for the toxic culture they had. Again, she wondered if she could be the instigator the women needed to bring attention to their unfair treatment. Of the boys in the mines , and the girl who couldn't talk. How many more were there who suffered injustice in this place?

When they reached the outer doors with the dragon etched into the metal, Ferrus told them to wait there for him to speak to the king first; then he would get them. After the doors closed behind the fae, Lilah ran her fingers over the design. The dragon was fierce-looking but weren't they all.

"Too bad you can't add that to your collection," Wren said. "It's really cool."

All her life, she'd loved anything to do with dragons. She watched Game of Thrones just to get a glimpse of their overgrown lizards. Something about this dragon was different. She'd noticed earlier that the monster didn't have wings. It was a mix of Godzilla and a T-Rex. More toward the Rex side, though.

One of the doors opened, and she stepped back, snatching her hand to her chest.

"All right," Ferrus said, "the King is ready." He zeroed in on her. "You talk through me."

"That's BS. There's no reason—" He lifted a finger, halting her tirade. "Fine. Just go." They followed him into the room where the king sat exactly as he was a few hours ago. Didn't look like he even moved.

"What is this I hear about an army?"

Lilah turned to Wren. "They let you out so you can tell Ferrus, here, about the guy you saw in the forest the day we abandoned the old village."

"Sure," Wren said, looking around Ferrus at the king.

"Wren, tell Ferrus, not the King," Lilah said with slight disgust in her voice.

"But the king asked—"

"I know," she said, lifting her hands, "I'll explain later." They all listened to Wren's story about meeting with the strange man. She left out the part about the gemstones. Right call on that. She didn't know if it would be advantageous to share that info or keep it to themselves for now.

Both Ferrus and the king sat thinking over what they had heard. The King asked, "So what creature or creatures make up the fighters."

Oh damn.

When Wren said *kappies,* the room exploded into laughter. Even the guards were laughing.

"Just because they are three feet tall doesn't mean they can't be dangerous. What if they have some super weapon you don't know about?" Suddenly, Lilah had all the attention on her. She swallowed hard. "I'm just sayin'."

Her stomach growled, and she was sure nobody had given Wren and her mate anything to eat or drink either. So when nobody said anything, she asked, "Can we go up to the kitchen to get something to eat?" She glowered at Ferrus. "Since I was occupied, we didn't get to eat." She wanted to check on the woman who was hit also. Make sure she was okay.

"Guards," the king hollered, "take the prisoners back to the holding cell."

"What?" Lilah yelled back. Ferrus started pushing her out of the room. Before he got the one door closed, Lilah had wrapped her fingers around the edge of the other door and pulled her head back in. "You have no right to imprison us. This is inhumane treatment."

Ferrus carefully pried at her fingers from around the door. Jerk. She saw the smile he was holding back.

"Ferrus," the king said, "stay." She didn't like the way that sounded. Almost threatening. Ferrus stiffened, hardening his face.

Fear zipped through her. "Why do you have to

stay? You're not in trouble, are you?" Through her mind scenes from movies where the hero was tied to a chair and had the living snot beat out of him until he was unconscious. That couldn't happen to Ferrus. "Tell him it was my fault."

The doors clanged closed.

Damn.

CHAPTER TEN

Tell him it was my fault.

Ferrus closed the doors to the throne room and smiled to himself. She was worried about him. She cared, though he bet she would not admit it to anyone, including herself. A warm flow filled his body in the chill of the room. His mate. What was he going to do with her?

"Ferrus," the king said. Ferrus turned to him from the entrance.

"Yes, My King."

His father stared at him with narrowed eyes. Dragon dicks, he showed too much happiness. His father knew him well enough to know when his moods were off. He kept his head bowed to hide his face.

"Ferrus, I do not have to remind you of the law against mates, do I?"

Though he did not want to, his animal took it as a direct threat to the one born just for them. His dragon wanted to eat the royal in one bite. No, make it two, so he would not wiggle going down its throat. Ferrus told his other side to stand down. They were not hurting the man who raised him.

"No My King." The long pause after his response unnerved him. He remained where he was before the ruler, with his head bowed. He knew what was expected of him. As the future leader of the clan, he had to do what was best for his people. And according to his father, mates were the destruction of a male's soul.

"Good, now what have you found out about our visitors." The king glanced to the side. "Come out of hiding, Ferra. I want to know what you have seen."

"Yes Father." His sister hurried from her usual perch in the darkest corner of the room, where she liked to eavesdrop when the king allowed. She was still too young to understand what the world was about. In a few peaks, she would be mating age, if such a thing had been allowed. He wanted her to be happy and thought many times about sending her away if she found her mate among the clan so she could live a normal life with him. But that put a knife through his heart just thinking about her gone.

"Ferrus, who are they, and where are they from?"

He paced as he ran the answers through his head, picking out which to share and what to keep to himself.

"The two non-gnoleon females I don't think are from our dimension."

"Why not," the king asked.

"Because the one with pale hair, she calls herself Lilah, has ideas about...certain things that few would allow on our planet. Unless there is some new advanced civilization, we don't know about."

"I doubt that seriously," the royal interjected.

Ferrus agreed. "As for why they are here, I'm not sure. But they were traveling to the town."

Ferra gasped. "What business would they have there? Only thieves and murderers seek such a place."

The town was known to be full of rogues and

killers who would do any job for payment. Those who managed to survive there worked the water ports where other lands came to barter and trade for goods. Many pilgrimages were made to the port town, where worshipers went to pray to the Mother of the Mountain at the Standing Stones.

Ferrus had been there a few times to study the creatures there to see if any were a possible threat to the citogen. None were, unless paid, and no one had enough wealth to convince an army to go against his warriors.

"I do not know what their business is in the town. They did not say."

"So, do they hold magic? Are they a threat to us?" his father asked.

Ferrus had to be so careful answering. If he said the wrong thing, he could doom his mate.

"No magic I detect," Ferra rushed out then turned toward him. He didn't look at her. They would talk afterward. "I do not think they mean us any harm. They are only females. What can they do? The male gnoleon with them seems quite capable, but he has no weapons." In fact, Ferrus sensed he was an alpha. But the male seemed too worried about his mate rather than presenting any danger to the citogen fae.

"Good," the king sighed, "we can send them on their way. That female—"

"No," Ferrus blurted, then added, "My King. I think they are worth examining a day or two longer. Just to make sure they are not concealing any crucial facts." Again, the king paused, studying his son.

The king cleared his throat. "Ferra, what are your observations?"

"They had plenty of chances to try to escape, yet they did not use force of any kind. They had a plan to tour our home to find an escape route. I say you should release them." She eyed her brother. He knew she had seen something she wasn't saying. Nonetheless, he growled at her opinion.

"No," she said, "I have changed my mind." Her smile to him turned devious. Oh, yes. She knew something good. "Perhaps they should stay for surveillance tonight." What was going through her mind? Ferra might have been young, but she thought as an adult.

"So be it. Ferrus, what of this Kappy army? I cannot believe a word of it." A partial grin appeared on the old man's face, more than he'd seen in centuries.

"I agree, Father. A Kappy army is nothing to

worry about. But somebody did set the forest on fire. The dark-magic smoke filling the sky that day was real."

"So, you believe the Gnoleon female about the village appearing nearby because of their evacuation? Not for war."

"I do believe that. Lilah said the same thing in so many words."

"Lilah?" the king questioned. Dragon piss! He needed to be more careful. If he seemed too comfortable, too personable with her, his father would suspect something. He hardened his face.

"Yes, My King, the one with the ugly hair with no color. She's the one who talks too much. Daphne is the taller, thin female. Wren is the one with darker skin." His dragon disagreed about Lilah's hair, but this was just a ploy to satisfy his father's curiosity.

"The matter is settled. Set up the females' rooms for tonight with the others." He stood with a slight groan, waving a dismissive hand. "Let the men select who stays with each tonight. I will be in my rooms." He shuffled to the back, slid open the wall, and closed it behind him.

Ferrus grabbed his sister's arm and hauled her

outside the throne room. She erupted into laughter. "You are in so much trouble."

His eyes squinted. "What do you mean?"

"I saw it," she said. "Lilah turned rock into metal. Only a female alpha can do that."

He stumbled backward, running his hand over his head. His mother was the only other person who could manipulate elements that way. A special magic only for the most powerful of the citogen.

"Does anyone else know this?" he asked.

"All the women in the kitchen at that time."

"Dragon balls!" He paced, worried about so many things at once. His mate, his men, his father. "Ferra, have you noticed a change in our father?"

"He gets tired easier and has less patience. He hardly comes out of his room anymore. I think he is getting tired of living."

Fear shot through him. Losing his mother at a young age crushed him. His father's passing would push him into a dark place. His father was too young to die. He was barely a thousand.

Ferra asked, "What are you going to do concerning your mate?"

"I cannot live without her," he answered.

"She cannot live *with* you. I fear for her. I think Father saw you when she entered the room with you. You did not take your eyes off her the entire time."

He knew he had given her away. His hands fisted into balls. His growl deepened. His animal would not let her be hurt by anyone, including the King.

He blew out a breath. "My mate needs food. I will figure it out later." Thoughts swirling in his head and fear in his heart, he started up the slope to the mountaintop and the food preparation area. The midday meal had been over for a while now. His men were probably wondering where he was. But there was no war coming, so they could sit on their asses as far as he was concerned at the moment.

When he reached the kitchen, he had to wait for his eyes to adjust to the brightness. The women were quite startled by his appearance. Many scrambled to put their coveralls on. Others dropped what they were doing and bowed with the usual "My Prince."

"I need the four visitors in the holding cell to have food and drink." He breathed in the fresh air. He'd forgotten how nice it was to be outside.

Instead of taking the tunnel that passed the

throne room, he took the way the men used when coming up to eat. He needed time to think.

Could he abandon everything he knew and loved to stay with his mate away from the mountain? Or would he force her to give up everything?

CHAPTER ELEVEN

L uzzeh Full continued to bash in the brains of his strategist on the cave floor in front of his makeshift throne. The stupid little piece of shit had utterly failed him. The villagers were gone with no sign of them anywhere.

He had no idea how they could've gotten away without being seen. The fire ate everything in its path, leaving only the dead ground behind. When searching the area, they found no sign of them. None! That wasn't possible.

He needed those portals stones from the three females. He would not remain in this goddess-forsaken dimension. Revenge would be his when he returned to the Crystal Kingdom. The fairy bitch would die. Then he would take over the fae king's people and live like a king with servers to satisfy his every desire and enough wealth to purchase more female servers to meet his needs. Only then would he be happy.

Where were those three girls? He must have them. He would do anything to get them.

"S-s-sire," a squeaky voice came from the entrance of the room.

He spun around, throwing his staff at the intruder.

"What?!" Luzzeh stomped toward his throne.

"One of the scouts has information for you." The scrawny-legged green creature shook.

"Send him in."

"Yes, sire," he replied, backing in a forward bent posture. When close enough to the door, he ran out. Worthless pieces of orc shit. At this rate, he was never getting out of this dimension. A kappy almost identical to the other walked in and bowed before him.

"Sire, the females have been seen climbing the citogen volcano."

"Who the demon's hell are the citogen?"

"They are the red fae warriors, sire."

"Warriors, you say?" He quickly calculated how

many of his own soldiers he'd lose if they battled. He figured twenty kappies per fae. Estimating one hundred men to keep the math simple, he'd lose over half his army. But if they captured the females, the number lost would mean nothing. His happy ass would be back in the Crystal Kingdom before the next meal.

The bowing kappy said, "Perhaps, sire, the citogen will negotiate with you for the females."

Negotiate? When was the last time he didn't just take all he wanted? But maybe this would be an excellent first step. He could scope out the enemy's offense, the enemy's stronghold.

Yes. He was brilliant.

Now to finally get those females.

CHAPTER TWELVE

L ilah paced behind the iron bars, furious
at being locked up again. They told the
king the truth about Zee's village
suddenly showing up, proving they were not the
enemy. But on the good side of this, she'd hopefully get to see Ferrus again.

He heated her body and her head. She was torn
between drooling over him and yelling at him.
Who did he think he was dropping the bomb in
the mine tunnel, demanding she was his? Like she
would consider being with a man who she couldn't
even show her body to.

Okay, she was kidding herself. She wanted to
be with him. Down and dirty, rolling in the mud

with him, but she couldn't see herself staying in this environment long term. Hot warrior or not.

Voices in the hallway startled her out of her daydreaming. She heard the male guard say, "I was not told about the prisoners being fed. You cannot enter." Softer words were spoken, arguing with the man.

Another male voice said, "Let them through. They are only females. They're useless against us."

Lilah's blood boiled, and she was about to pop her top. If these men said one more degrading remark to a woman, she'd take on her first case of sex discrimination in this strange world.

Around the corner came Valori and Shinni carrying large trays with food and jugs of water. Thank god! Ferra came forward and gripped the bars, bending them enough to pass the dishes through.

"Thank you so much, Valori and Shinni," Daphne said. "I'm starving." The group of four sat and handed around the bowls. The food resembled a leafy salad with strips of orange, yellow, and brown. Another stone container held diced purple pieces. They reminded her of beets and passed them on.

Ferra gave Valori a look that said something was up.

"What?" Lilah said. "If you need to say something, say it."

The three ladies sat in front of the group on the outside of the bars.

"Lilah," Valori said. She glanced at the woman, seeing the concern in her caring face. "You changed rock into metal."

Wren sat up. "Really? That's awesome. How'd you do that?"

Lilah lifted a shoulder and dropped it. "Not sure. It's probably like you making trees from chairs and tables." She hadn't compared herself to her cousin, but her ability was sorta like Wren's. The normal gnoleon couldn't control limbs and roots. Her cousin was the alpha female, the only one who had the power—

A thought hit her, and she gasped, sucking her food down the wrong pipe. Slapping her hand on her chest, she coughed up a piece of leaf.

Daphne pounded on her back. "You okay?"

Still coughing, she shook her head, then took a breath. "Not if they're going to tell me what I think they are."

Daphne frowned, brows drawn. "What are they telling you?"

Lilah stared the elder in the eye. "Let me guess. Only the female alpha is able to make stone into metal." All three women bowed their heads.

"Yes, Alpha," the trio said in unison.

Lilah dropped her carrot-looking thing. "Whoa, whoa, whoa, ladies. There will be none of that bowing stuff. I'm the same as you." Well, Lilah wasn't really like anyone else there unless someone liked to argue points of law and precedence.

But she did *look* like them, heavy hips and ass from walking the slopes their entire lives, the same idea as Wren resembling the villagers in the forest and her alpha mate.

Wren and Daphne stopped eating to stare at her. "You are the mate to the next in line to be king? Just like me?" Wren's smile lit up her face for the first time since they got here.

Oh shit. She dropped her face into her hands, her cheeks heating quickly. Who was the prince? Ferrus said the asshole who hit the woman in the dining room was the prince. That was precisely what she'd expect from this king's son.

Valori whispered, "This is very dangerous for you because mates are not allowed."

That didn't make sense. "Mates are mates, allowed or not. As far as I know." She glanced at Zee.

He tilted his head to the right. "That is how I understand the mating call."

"No, not like that," Valori continued. "Mates are not allowed to be together, or the female will be killed."

Lilah's jaw fell open. "You've got to be fucking kidding? Of course, it would be the female." Her hands squeezed whatever food she had in it. She wanted to throw it against the wall to express her frustration, but that would be childish. As an adult, she could control her actions.

Valori continued. "In the years following the no mates dictate, there had been attacks on females. Most were of the sexual kind. To not tempt men, the king ordered females to hide their bodies."

Lilah let out a deep breath. One more negative thing, and that would be it. Her top would flip. "Okay, so we can't tell anyone, or I'll be killed. We'll never be together." She sighed with relief, knowing she wouldn't have to be with that bastard, but her heart hitched at the thought of not seeing Ferrus again.

She barely knew him, but she wanted to be with

him. And no—she was sure she'd never *be* with him. He was an angelic face and could have any of the beautiful women here whenever he wanted. She'd seen children, so apparently, sex was still approved.

"Oh," Shinni said, "you will get to see him at night."

"I don't understand. Is the rule suspended at night?"

The younger one's face turned bright red.

Valori harrumphed at the younger fae. "According to law, when it is time to rest for the night, each male chooses a female to sleep with. Whether they join for bearing a child or not does not matter. As long as the male is able to satisfy their inner urges is what matters."

"Uh, hold on a minute," Lilah let those words roll around in her head. She knew she heard them wrong. "Could you please expand on what you're saying."

Shinni leaned closer to the bars and whispered, "Those who are mates—the males spend the night with their mates in her room."

Daphne glanced at her with a frown. Her cousin said, "I thought I heard something about men *deciding* who they sleep with?"

Fuck. Lilah knew she heard that too. But she needed to verify just to make sure.

"Valori, are you saying the women have no say in whether they want to sleep alone or who sleeps with them?" She tried like hell to keep her voice steady.

"Hey," the guard shouted from the entrance, "you females be quiet. You shouldn't be talking anyway. Don't you have something to do except gab all day?"

Lilah's jaw clenched. That was it. She couldn't stand it anymore. She breathed in deeply, expelling the fury inside her chest little by little.

"Valori," Daphne said, "you cannot live like that. If the woman doesn't want sex and the man makes her, that's called rape, which is punished severely where we come from."

Lilah had calmed enough to speak. "You have to put a stop to it. All of it. The cover-ups, the oppression, rape, and the boys in the mine. Oh my god. I forgot about them." She took another breath. "Valori, women receive no respect here. The men are taking advantage of you in every way they can. It has to stop."

Valori's eyes widened. "It's the king's rule. How

am I to go against the king? They will have me punished."

Lilah thought about the circumstances. What would she suggest if her client wasn't able to get away from the injustice? In the past, she had driven to a woman's home to help her escape an abusive situation. It didn't seem like a big deal until her car was shot at. But she got the abuser on a prior and domestic abuse charges, which put him away for a max of five years.

That's what they needed, someone to help them get away. To escape. But where would they all stay? She turned to Zee with a smile.

"Ladies," Lilah said, "let me introduce you to the alpha of the forest dwellers. They have a very lovely new home. Would you like to visit?"

CHAPTER THIRTEEN

L ilah paced outside the jail cell. While the guard they had tied up and gagged sat glowering at her from inside the bars.

"Stop staring at me like you want to chop my head off. We're going on strike for your own good. You'll thank me later." The guard mumbled, and she was sure he said something along the lines of he wasn't buying it. "Send someone to the forest dwellers' village when the king wants to talk about changes that *must* be made before we come back."

Valori hurried around the corner with a few sleepy-eyed boys who still had dust on their clothes. "This is everyone. Let's go."

Holding a torch, Ferra led the group down the tunnel from the holding room. Down, down,

down. Lilah wondered if they were going down to the lava pits again. She looked around to make sure the young lady she met there was in the group. The girl was up in front with a few others following along.

Finally, they slowed as they came to a dead-end rock wall.

What the hell? All this way just to go back?

Ferra placed the torch in a holder then placed her hands side by side on the wall. As she pushed her hands to both sides, the wall split and slid to the side just like yanking open a set of curtains. Lilah couldn't keep her jaw closed. Seeing it up close was fascinating. Though it was probably easy for them, it looked like a miracle, like Moses splitting the water of the Red Sea.

On the other side stood a grinning Xenos and Wren. Valori had snuck them out earlier to alert the village of their arrival. A few Gnoleon women were there also. When the first of the Citogen stepped out, brown fae and red fae stared at each other.

Was this the first time the two species had met? She hadn't thought about how they would react to each other. Would their coloring define how they felt about each other?

Xenos pulled his sister Iridia, the leader of the Gnoleon, to his side and introduced her to Ferra. The significance of this meeting wasn't lost on Lilah. These two were the next generation of leaders among their people. They would shape the future, and that forthcoming time would be based on what happened in the next twenty-four to forty-eight hours.

God, Lilah hoped this was the right move. If not, she single-handedly doomed an entire female population to a living hell.

Ferra and Iridia motioned the group forward, and quietly, they disappeared into the forest on the trek to the village. The sun hadn't topped the horizon yet, but the first rays had lit the sky. The air was crisp and invigorating. Energy and excitement rolled through her. The only thing that could've made it better was to have Ferrus with her.

She stopped in her tracks. That thought was unexpected. She searched her heart and realized it was true. The man wasn't as bad as she had made the males out to be in her mind. He was nothing like the asshole in the dining room, the prince. Ferrus seemed like any other guy on Earth. Except he was nice to her.

But he hadn't done anything to stop the injustices the females had been enduring for years. But as a lowly warrior, how could he help with change? He didn't see his home as the toxic environment that it was. It was what he was used to. He wasn't experiencing the bad. Well, if he mediated between her and the king, he'd know exactly what the problems were. He'd know what needed to change, and what needed to happen now.

Lilah would stand for these women who didn't have a voice in their lives. She would make sure the children, girls and boys, didn't suffer as their mothers had.

By the time Lilah reached the village, some were already mingling. She noted that many of the red Fae Citogen had brought stone bowls and dishes and kitchen knives. The Gnoleon village was in the middle of preparing breakfast, and the visiting women jumped right in.

The mountain women marveled over the berries and nuts that the forest held. She heard Valori say that she remembered eating the exotic foods when she was little. For some reason, no one came out to collect such delicacies any longer. Lilah doubted the king would let them out to gather anything.

Iridia told her that she was welcome to gather at any time. In fact, the female alpha said she would have the gardeners plant several of the bushes on the forest perimeter to the mountain, so they had easy access. They would make sure every year that the plants remained healthy and abundant just in case the Mother of the Land needed a little help.

The Citogen stared at Iridia. "Do you mean Mother of the Mountain?"

The female alpha tipped her head to the left. "No. Mother of the Land."

Valori smiled. "We need to share stories on our beginnings. I think we may find many similarities."

Lilah moved through the village to see how the rest of the Citogen were. If the tension was thick somewhere, she was the one to smooth things over. Oddly enough, she found Ferra surrounded by men and their weapons.

The girl appeared to be a little young to look for a mate, maybe in a couple years. At the rate they were going, it wouldn't matter if she found a mate or not. She'd be condemned to no love or joy.

Ferra held an arrow with a stone arrowhead the forest people used to hunt. The edges were sharp, as sharp as rock pounding on a rock could get. Ferra pinched the edges between two fingers and ran them around the perimeter of the triangle. When she pulled her hand away, the edges were razor sharp and smooth. The men gasped and pushed all of their arrows at her to do. The girl laughed. That was something Lilah hadn't seen from the princess. Happiness.

Down the way, she heard Shinni's voice. Lilah wandered toward the edge of the village where the gardens were. Several of the men and women from both sides were gathered around a section of dirt where the Gnoleon demonstrated how their magic worked with the plants.

Lilah watched as one of the Gnoleon women buried a seed then placed her hand on top of the dirt. Within seconds, a green sprout popped out of the soil. The Citogen gasped just like the Gnoleon had with Ferra.

Peace settled in her heart. She was confident this was the best thing she could've done for the red fae—technically, her people. That thought nearly knocked her on her ass. *Her* people, if she chose for them to be.

Xenos had given his right to rule to his sister so he could stay with Wren as they trekked to the Island of the Standing Stones. Lilah would do the same and stay the hell away from the mountain. But what about the women and children? As soon as she left, would they go back to the way things were? Absolutely they would. She already knew.

She had to choose whether to sacrifice her happiness and stay to ensure the women were treated fairly, or to run away and hate herself for the rest of her life for being a wussy.

But what if she didn't tell the prince who she was. Maybe she could stay but be an "unmated" female. That way, she could see Ferrus. As long as he was unmated. Shit. She had no idea if he was single. He'd spoken with her, and he looked like he wanted to eat her, but that was something a male would do on any planet, coupled or not. Her heart cracked.

She couldn't stay if he was mated to someone else. Seeing him with his mate would crush Lilah. Unrequited love was the worst thing ever. Whoa, who said anything about love? She was just interested, that's all. Even though no one had intrigued her as much as that man did. No one looked as delicious as that man did. She knew she'd dream of him every night.

She noticed that he stared at her a lot. She loved having his attention on her. When they were in the tunnel, so close together, yet not, he smelled so good, like crisp, clean air. And the fact that soldiers wore little clothing did nothing to help her libido.

She imagined her hands sliding over his well-formed pecs. Down his ripped stomach and over his thick cock. She could feel her breasts mashed against his chest, his breath on her face. She fanned her face and glanced around, hoping no one noticed. But the daydream didn't end there.

Lilah imagined his hands running up her hips and around her back. His cock nestled at the junction of her thighs, and she could feel the wetness running down her legs. She really needed to see him again and prove to herself he was as hot as she imagined.

Mates. The thought warmed her soul. The only mate experience she had was what she saw at the tree village. She looked around. Everyone seemed to be in love with the person they stood with. Men and women worked side by side, flirting and smiling, and looking happy. Nobody in the mountain seemed even close to that.

Iridia, the Gnoleon alpha female, stopped beside her, watching the scene in the garden. "It is good you brought our new neighbors to visit. Learning new ways is always good."

"Well, there's another reason than purely social." She wondered if she should share with Iridia the problems she sought to make right. "The mountain fae live very differently than you do. I think seeing your culture and how you all work together will be good for them. Right now, women are not seen as equals."

"I see," the alpha said. "Then it is excellent that you brought them here. We will welcome them as long as they need to stay."

"There will be someone from the mountain men coming to talk about changing things. I don't know when he will be here, but if your guards could refrain from killing him, that would be great."

With a smile, Iridia bowed her head. "I will make certain of his survival." As she stepped away, Lilah called her back.

"Iridia, what can you tell me about mates?" When the woman's face lit up, Lilah didn't want her to know why she was asking. "You know, what should we expect from Wren and your brother as time goes on?"

"They are the same as all other mates. They will

love each other and no other for the rest of their lives."

"So, Zee—sorry—Xenos won't get bored and look for excitement elsewhere?"

"No. Never has that happened. In truth, when one mate goes to the spirit—" Lilah figured that meant 'dead'—"the other often decides to retire."

"Retire as in goes to the spirit," she asked. Iridia tilted her head to the right, which Lilah remembered was their way of saying yes. So instead of staying alive and looking for another love, they would rather die. "No matter what their mate looks like, they stay in love?"

Iridia smiled and looked away. Crap. Lilah knew she'd give herself away with that question.

"Alpha female," Iridia said to her. How did she know? Did one alpha recognize another? "The mating call has no eyes or ears or nose. Only a heart that knows its other half when it sees it."

Lilah asked, "So they are perfect for each other? They will never argue or disagree?"

The leader laughed. "Oh, I did not say that. Each mate has their own will, but when it comes to respect and love, they are perfect."

"Xenos will never break Wren's heart?"

Iridia tilted her head again. "Never from not loving her or being faithful."

Lilah let out a breath. "That's good to know. Thanks."

"You are welcome." She smiled. "*Wren* is safe."

Lilah wasn't sure she could believe what the Gnoleon said. But the woman had no reason to lie to her. And what she'd seen for herself correlated. But if she was supposed to be mated to the heir, why did she feel nothing but disgust for him?

"One last question," Lilah said quickly. "Is the mating call ever wrong when matching couples?"

"Never."

CHAPTER FOURTEEN

Shinni's high-pitch squeal drew her attention. Iridia joined the gardeners. The seedling they had planted a bit ago had grown tall with green bean-like things hanging from the stalk. Lilah had little doubt that the mountain men were going to have more variety in their menu.

Shinni saw Lilah watching and joined her. Lilah wasn't much into growing things. All the plants she'd ever had died from drowning. She was always afraid the flower wasn't getting enough water. But she should spend time learning all she could if she were to help these women.

When Lilah came to stand next to Shinni, the fae bowed her head to Lilah, then waved over the red fae in the garden group. The happy fae introduced her to the women, Lilah running their names and faces through her mind to memorize both. When they bowed their heads and said *We are honored*—Lilah stopped them right there.

Shinni had been in the holding room when Lilah said she didn't want any royal treatment. She meant it. But her red friend pulled her away from the group.

"Alpha," Shinni said, and Lilah opened her mouth to set her straight, but the woman continued, "if you please, you should reconsider your thoughts about not being treated as you should be."

"But I'm nothing special—"

"No, you are special, Alpha. Look where we are, what we are doing. Do you think any of us could accomplish this? We haven't in hundreds of peaks, and we wouldn't in a hundred more."

"What's a peak exactly?" She didn't mean to change the subject. Wait, yes, she did.

Shinni frowned at her. Guess she wasn't being subtle enough.

"A peak is when the sun rises directly in line with the highest peak on our mountain range. We gauge age and the passage of time that way."

Oh, that made sense. "Like the solstices where I come from."

"So, Alpha mate…" Damn, the diversion didn't work. "let us once again have a royal female to look up to. Someone we can go to with problems or just to talk. We haven't had that in such a long time."

"What happened to your queen?" Lilah had wondered why she had seen only the king.

Shinni dropped her chin to her chest. "Our beloved queen died of a mysterious illness. Complications were sudden and unexpected."

Her heart broke for the woman. Apparently, they truly cared for their rulers and didn't see them as tyrants. Well, except for the current king. Lilah opened her arms and hugged the fae. She felt a bond form between her and Shinni, a shift in her soul that connected with the fae. Lilah could sense her fae's sadness and the growing feeling of hope.

How could that be? She'd hugged people for years and had never felt this way. Maybe it was because, in her heart, she'd accepted being the woman they needed. She would be their alpha female.

"All right. You win," Lilah replied. "I'll be the person to go to when things go wrong. If that means y'all have to bend forward when seeing me, so be it." She pulled away and saw Shinni's smile. "That's what I like to see."

Tears shined in the red-tinted eyes. "You will make a wonderful alpha mate." The frown returned. "As long as the king doesn't kill you for being a mate. We must keep you a secret from him."

And the prince. She blew out a breath. "That's a problem."

"But that's why we're here, right? For the men to understand, we aren't "just females." That we do a lot for our people and deserve respect. We're not something they can use as they wish. You're doing the right thing, Alpha."

Lilah almost cried from the belief and trust this fae gave her. The magnitude of what she was doing hit her again. But she felt comforted that at least one person thought she was on track with her actions.

The other three women with Shinni stared at her with reverence. "Alpha, we want you to know that we are thankful for your help. This will be good for all the women."

"You're welcome. Hopefully, it will be good for the boys too."

"What boys?" Shinni asked.

"Those in the mines who breathe in the dust all day. All that has to be stopped."

Shinni replied, "The dust is from mountain rock. It is good to breathe. It builds a strong body."

"That can't be right," Lilah said. "The men are just saying that so the boys keep doing the grunt work."

"Alpha," Shinni pleaded, "the mountain, the stone, is a part of us as we are a part of it. We crush stone for many things. We breathe in the dust. It makes us all stronger."

"She is correct." Valori joined them. "The rock is essential to our lives. Only strong alphas can be gone long from the rock. We use it in our foods and medicinal needs." While the elder spoke, the others returned to the garden. Valori put a hand on the arm of the young lady who made the swords in the lava pits.

"Alpha, this is Muriel. She had a strange sickness as a child that took away her ability to speak."

Lilah smiled. "Yes, we met earlier." As with the others, Lilah gave her a hug initiating their female bond. When she pulled back, Muriel's eyes were wide. Had she felt the link too?

Valori continued. "Muriel wants you to know about the ash."

"Ash?"

"Yes. It's not a secret among the females, but she wants our alpha female to know. When melting down the rock the boys put into the cauldron—"

The scene in the lava pit popped into Lilah's head. "That's what you were doing down there? Melting rocks?"

"Yes. That is how we make the metal items we use. Small particles of iron are mixed with the stone. Only the lava is hot enough to melt the hard material, releasing the metal in a liquid state. It floats to the top, and Muriel pours it into shaped casts. Rock ash is left behind, which she dumps before starting the procedure again."

"Got it," Lilah replied. She wondered what else she didn't know about these people. There was so much to learn. "Now, what about the ash?"

"It is important that you know this. When mixing the metal with a bit of ash, the metal becomes much stronger and can be filed down to a sharp blade."

"Like your kitchen knives," Lilah said. She

remembered the knives were shiny, and the swords were not.

"Yes," Valori added. "Muriel made those for us. She combined the ash and sharpened them to the point they would cut rock."

"Yowzer," Lilah replied. "I can see myself slicing all my fingertips off." She rubbed her fingers against her palms. "So why are the swords not shiny like your knives?"

Both fae's expressions turned angry. "Because the smith refuses to take the time to understand her. Even when I told him about this, he chose to ignore it, saying a female wasn't smart enough to know that. He would never let her make the mixture."

"Do you use the knives to protect yourselves?" Lilah wondered if this could be a way for the ladies to remind the men they weren't in charge anymore. A little nick on the arm would be a good equalizer.

"No," Valori answered. "We have our nibblers for that."

"A what?" Lilah hadn't heard that word before.

Valori and Muriel reached under their blanket coveralls and pulled out gadgets that basically were rock slings. Lilah didn't know whether to laugh or be afraid for their safety.

Muriel loaded her sling with a rock, then twirled the long strings at her side, building speed and momentum as it circled around and around. With a flip of her wrist, the rock shot out like from a gun. She aimed at a gourd sitting on the ground by the garden. Next thing Lilah knew, the gourd exploded like a bomb had been inside it. Flecks of mushed melon rained down. If that had been someone's head, the mush matter would've been made of brains. Eww.

"Does everyone have one of those?" she asked.

"Only the females. We carry them at all times."

Lilah smirked. "I bet the men think those are useless, right?"

Valori and Muriel looked at each other than at her. "How did you know?"

Lilah winked at them. "I'm the alpha female, yes?"

One of the Gnoleon had noticed the weapon exhibition. "Do that again," he said. "That was amazing." He put a smaller melon on a stump.

Valori pulled out her nibbler, loaded a rock into the pouch, and swirled it until it spun so fast it was a blur. She flicked her wrist, and a blink later, the gourd had a single hole in the front. The man lifted the melon and turned it. The entire backside had blown out. Once again, the fallout would've been brain matter.

Okay, she had to admit she wasn't all that worried about their safety anymore. She really needed to learn how to work the sling. Seemed easy, but so did writing a book.

She hoped that Ferrus was the one to come and negotiate. But it would probably be the prince, not a warrior trained to fight. She sighed, thinking of Ferrus. She would've chosen him over the asshole prince any day. If she ever saw him again, she'd take the time to get to know him. Would he be interested in her? How could he?

She still had the same problems she had in school when it came to boys. If that was the case, he wouldn't even give her a chance. Or if he did, it was because rumors said she was easy. She was quick to let the boys know she wasn't. And that was that.

She'd end up alone again.

CHAPTER FIFTEEN

Ferrus rolled and turned all night, unable to sleep. He wanted his mate, but he couldn't have her. He could not even talk to her without his father becoming more suspicious. She was so beautiful, so perfect. Even when arguing, she turned him on. Her face tinted red when she was angry, making her stunning.

He couldn't think straight when she was close. She smelled so good—like water from the snow caps, fresh and clean.

The way she had come to the aid of the woman Silvo struck at the midday meal was amazing. She was brave, confident, strong. She challenged Silvo with only her eyes, making the warrior back down.

She was a perfect alpha mate, the ideal queen for him when the time came.

The sun had been up for a time. The early meal should be ready soon. He got up and dressed in long pants he wore when not training. He seldom wore shirts as they restricted his movements when it came to using his sword. A good warrior was always battle-ready.

Despite what the king had commanded, their two strange females had not been set up in their own rooms. He made the order to the female elder. He hadn't wanted to kill one of his men for thinking they could touch his mate, but if he claimed her, then his father would know for certain she was his mate. With the two staying in the holding room, all of that was avoided. But he still wanted to be beside her.

Maybe if he wandered straight to the cells, he could at least see her for a moment. Her friends would be with her, but he'd be in the same room as she was. He bolted from his room to the tunnel that led to the rod cell then eventually to the hidden escape.

When he approached, he wondered why the guard wasn't at his post. Entering the room, he saw his sentry tied up and on the inside of the cell. And no Lilah.

In a panic, he ripped the bars apart to get to the male.

"Where are the females?" he asked as he pulled the gag from the soldier's mouth.

"They left. Said they were going on strike, whatever that means."

Ferrus sat back on his ass. "They are gone?" He would never see her again. His animal cried out in his head. If he were to leave now, he could catch up to her, and they could go together to her destination. He would keep her safe and with him.

"How long ago did she leave?" he asked.

"My prince, I don't think you understand. They *all* left. The females and children went to the tree lovers in the forest. The one with the loud mouth said you needed to go talk to her when you were ready to make changes."

"Changes? What changes?"

The warrior's cheeks turned redder than the rest of his face. "I overheard them talking about how we treated the women. They want equality. They are basically useless to us, and they are mad about that. I can't see how it's *our* fault they aren't worth much in protecting our home."

Mother of the Mountain! His mate was beautiful, smart, and sneaky. But if the king didn't like her to begin with, this would push him to the edge. He helped his man with the binds and then paced for a moment.

She'd said to go to her when the males were ready for change. Demon's hell! If that were the case, he'd never see her again. It was too late to smooth this over. Even if he got all the women back, the king would find out who the instigator was. That couldn't happen. His father would not touch her.

His stomach growled. The early meal! With the women gone, no one was there to make their food. Oh, dragon balls, this was going to be very, very bad.

He rushed up the passage to the eating room to find the men milling about, confused about what was happening. "Where is our food?"

Ferrus's brow raised. Lesson number one, the women fed them and took care of all the food.

"Warriors to me." He went into the room with tables and chairs set up for them. Would the women demand to eat at the same time or afterward? When did they eat now? They had to eat sometime.

When the males had settled, he wasn't sure how to approach this in a way they would understand. "Warriors," he started, "the females have left to tend to female things." He knew anything related personally to females scared the dragon shit out of the males.

"All of them? What about our food?" one of his men asked.

"Well," he said, "guess we have to make it ourselves."

The room became utterly silent, not one belch or fart from any of them. Glancing over the group, he realized his soldiers were stunned and maybe a bit afraid.

Ferrus sighed. "Soldiers, the females are not here to take care of us. They are only coming back if we agree to treat them fairly. For too long, we have taken advantage of their kindness. If you believe the females to be useless, I think you're about to find out exactly how 'useless' they are. Everyone to the food prep cave."

He heard grumbles, curse words, and even a "where is the food prep cave" comment. He led them down the hallway where the light brightened with each step.

One of his men asked, "Where is that light

coming from? How did they get so much of it inside?"

Ferrus stepped into the food area to see the females had taken pity on them. The center section was filled with food but in its raw form. The men would have to cut and slice and figure out how to make this stuff edible. Oh Mother, they were going to starve to death.

"Hey, look at these knives. Ow, dragon piss, they're sharp." He heard a tapping sound. "And they are harder than a gunder tit in the snow. How did the females get these?"

"Where does this slope go? Kappy shit, I didn't know we had a garden. How did the females get the crops so large?"

"Mother of the Mountain, they have a water pool to relax in. Damnation, it's cold. How did the females get fresh water up here?"

"Why are there clothes over here? All of mine are dirty. How do the females know who these belong to?"

"I want to help prepare food from now on. It's nice up here."

"We can use giant reflectors to get light to the main cavern. How did the females know how to do this?"

It seemed he and his men could learn a few things from the females.

"Warriors, gather around." When the group settled, he gave instructions. "Now that we know the females are smarter than we thought, we need to use all this until they return. There is food on the center table. Cut it up, wash it, do whatever is needed to make it edible. I need to speak with the king."

CHAPTER SIXTEEN

Ferrus left the food prep area, hoping it would be intact when he returned. This thing, strike, was disturbing. The females had never done anything like this. What changed so much now, that the way they had been living for hundreds of peaks was so bad?

His father would not be pleased. He would be furious enough to send the army after them. If he knew where they were. Only Ferrus and the guard that had been locked in the cell were privy to their location.

He entered the throne room to see his father pulling the food cart into his private chambers. Thank the goddess, the women at least prepared his food, smart thinking on their part not to enrage the king with an empty stomach.

"Ferrus," his father said, "why aren't you with your men. Just because we are not going to war does not mean we get lazy."

"Father," he snarled, politely, "if I were lazy, I would still be in bed." With his mate, preferably. "We have a situation."

"You take care of it, Ferrus. I am sure you can manage an argument between two warriors."

"No, Father..." he sighed. "The females have gone."

The old man looked up at him. "Explain. Gone where?"

Fear crept inside his head. He knew who started all this, and his father would come down hard on her. "The females are not happy and have gone to visit," not the correct term, but it would do, "the forest dwellers."

"Well, go bring them back," the king said like there was little thought needed for that decision.

"They will not come back until things have changed."

A spark flickered through his father's eyes. His heart flipped. The man needed to remain calm. He did not want to fight the male. He was old and weak.

"What do they want to change?" the royal asked.

"I am not sure exactly. But the word *equality* was used."

His father snorted. "Why should they be equal when they do not equally share male responsibilities? We fight for them. We die for them. How can they think they are equal?" He shook his head. "Find out what it will take to get them back here and report to me."

"Yes, Father." Ferrus bowed and headed back to the food prep to instruct Silvo to continue training with the men until he returned.

AFTER FERRUS LEFT the throne room, the king sighed and leaned against the throne. The females. He couldn't deal with them. He couldn't even look at them.

A knock came from the main entrance. He just wanted to eat his morning meal in peace.

"What is it?" the king called.

One of his soldiers poked his head in. "Sire, you have a visitor."

At this time of the morning? "Tell them to come back later."

"Your Highness, he travels from far away to negotiate with you."

That caught his interest. "Give me a moment."

"Yes, Majesty." The guard ducked out and closed the main door. The king slipped off his lounging attire and put on his royal robes, grabbing a piece of bread before re-entering the chamber.

"You may enter," he commanded. The door opened, and a fae-like creature he had never seen walked in. The visitor's skin was pale, but he looked to be in good health. He wore strange garments made of fur he did not recognize. But what struck him the most was the dark magic swirling around the male.

The guest bowed his head. "I am Luzzeh Full, ruler of the kappies."

The king's brows rose. "The kappies have no leader."

"They do now. They follow my orders."

Interesting. This male who looked from another place had chosen the weakest creatures to gather for an army. With the magic surrounding the male, the king would have thought better decisions would have been made. Not everyone was capable of harnessing the evil power.

"What is it you want, Luzzeh?"

"I am looking for three females."

Was he thinking of starting a harem? "I have many females who would excite a male for the right price."

The leader frowned. "No, I'm looking for a specific trio." He abruptly stopped. The first thing that entered the king's mind was the three females his men had captured trespassing. Why these specific females.

"Who are they to you?" he asked his visitor.

The darkness around the man thickened as he expressed a sad illusion on his face. "These are my daughters. They have left the safety of my home after an argument with their mother." Luzzeh smiled. "You know how younglings are."

"Indeed, I do."

The king knew the male was lying. Apparently, the visitor did not know fae could see the negative energy around him. But this brought an opportunity that had not occurred to him before now.

He had not missed how his son doted on the

light-haired female. The boy could not take his eyes from her when they were here in the chamber. Though his son denied being attracted to the female, he knew. He had a mate once too. Those memories tried to surface, but he shut them down fiercely. Mates were strictly forbidden.

"Luzzeh, three females from another land are visiting us. I feel certain these are your *daughters* as they are different from anyone I have met."

"Yes," Luzzeh said, "that would be them. Strange clothing to you and words you don't know."

That was a perfect description. The loud female said, "inhumane," which he had never heard.

Luzzeh bowed his head. "Your Majesty, most powerful of all, if you would hand them over to me, I will take them home, and you can be done with them."

That would be good, he thought. He could get rid of the female Ferrus was fond of. "What have you in exchange for the females?"

"Exchange?" Luzzeh asked.

The king laughed. "You do not think I would give them to you for nothing in return, do you? What kind of ruler do you think I am?"

The male grumbled to himself. "Yes, you are

right, Your Highness. I will return and bring with me something you would never expect."

Pleased, the king dismissed him to come back later. Hopefully, by then, the three girls would be back for him to hand over while his son was none the wiser.

CHAPTER SEVENTEEN

Ferrus hurried from his home through the forest, following the scent of his females and mate. He was baffled by the reason for the females leaving. No one had complained before about anything. Why now?

He was afraid he knew the reason, his mate. The king would see her as a troublemaker and would not allow her back. His animal growled at the thought. *Ours.* What was the deal with mates that his dragon was adamant about keeping her?

His father never talked about having a mate. His mother had been gone for so long, he barely remembered what her face looked like. He recalled there was love and happiness between his parents, but he couldn't bring any specific memory to mind.

Soon after their mother died, the king ordered that being with a mate was not allowed. If caught together, the female would face consequences as strong as death. Ferrus had not seen the reason at that time, nor did he now.

He felt the mating pull, there was no doubt about that. But he knew so little about his mate. Outwardly, she seemed perfect—gorgeous body, silky pale hair. She looked like she belonged to their fae. Even her heart was with his fae. He knew she was doing this for the good of the females.

He thought back to the time he followed his mate to the mines. She said the females had to cover themselves while the men did not. What she did not understand was that men could not control themselves when seeing the females.

A strange scent floated in the air. He heard a twang, then a wood arrow embedded itself in the ground between his feet.

"I come to speak with the female who brought the mountain fae to your village. I carry no weapon and mean no harm to you." He lifted his arms and turned in a circle to show he was not hiding anything.

A dark-skinned male dropped right in front of him and sniffed. "You are from the mountain?"

"Yes." He wondered if it was safe to stay with the truth. Lilah trusted these fae enough to bring the females there, so they must be worthy. "My mate is here in your home."

The Gnoleon relaxed. "You seek the female humans. Yes, they are here. Follow me." Ferrus hurried to keep up with the male.

"Humans?" he questioned. He hadn't heard a fae of that calling.

The tree fae smiled. "Ask your mate. She will tell you a good story."

Story? What kind of life had his mate lived? They had to be advanced if the females had as much dominance as she seemed to have. Their warriors were probably brave since she had no fear of consequences. He wondered how different his mate's society must have been from his.

He saw a mound of dirt piled up taller than he was. Then he saw another one attached to the first, forming a highly defensible blockade against someone passing. Were they going to climb it, or was there an entrance elsewhere? His guide walked straight to the point where the mounds met.

As Ferrus watched, the Gnoleon put his hand

on the mound, and *the dirt moved*. The domes separated, allowing them passage. In a way, it was how the mountain fae opened and closed entrances for privacy. They just put their hands on the rock wall and pulled to each side or pushed them together.

Maybe the red and brown fae were not that different. Then Ferrus stepped beyond the dome and knew he was in a different world than his own. He truly hoped his scouts were correct that there were no stockpiles of weapons for battle.

As he continued to follow the guard, he took in all around him. Males and females worked side by side. Several, including his own females, worked with what could have been food, washing and cutting with primitive knives. His people could make blades for them to make prep easier. Did he just think about supplying possible enemies with weapons?

Movement beside him startled him. A male stood in the opening of a mound. He saw items inside that were of a personal nature. Was that where the fae slept as well as being a protective wall? Most impressive.

"Alpha," the guard hollered, "your visitor is here for the humans."

The tasks that were being done came to a sudden stop, and everybody stared at him.

"Ferrus!" He heard his name in his mate's voice. His heart did a strange thump in his chest. He searched the crowd, needing to see her. He wanted to have her in his arms. He could not believe he felt like this. He would think about it later. Right now, he wanted his mate.

Lilah pushed her way through the fae staring at him. "Ferrus," she called to him. And then she was there, right in front of him. She slowed, but he stepped forward, wrapped his arms around her, and lifted her off the ground. She squeaked, and he laughed. She was so adorable and felt so good against him.

He had not been hugged since he was a child. Her smell, her breasts, all of her pressed against him. Desire, like he had never known, set his body on fire. His dragon was happy. He wanted to take her in one of these mounds and mate her.

No. Mates were not allowed.

His animal breathed fire, ready to fight.

He set his mate on the ground but did not want to let go of her. Was what he was feeling true for all men with their mates? Demon's hell. He could barely control himself.

"Hello, Ferrus."

Ferrus looked up to see the male who occupied the holding cell not long ago. "I am Xenos, alpha, in name only, of the Gnoleon."

If not for holding on to his mate, Ferrus would have fallen on his ass from surprise. He had the leader of their one-time enemy in his hands. How ironic. Well, two could play that game. He did not think the tree alpha knew who he really was.

"Yes," Ferrus said with a smile, "I remember you. I am Ferrus, warrior of the Citogen." Both men nodded once. "What do you mean by 'alpha in name only'?"

Zee put his arm around a female that wasn't his mate and brought her forward. "I am leaving with my mate. My sister, Iridia, is the true alpha of the fae."

This time, Ferrus's legs did weaken. He started to fall backward, but Lilah kept hold of him. His mate scrunched her face. "You're thinking you can't believe that a female is leading a people, aren't you?"

He turned his eyes to her. How the demon's hell did she know that? Did she have dark magic that let her into his mind?

"See, Ferrus," she griped, "that right there is the

root of your men's issues. You don't believe women are capable of doing the same thing men are. I got news for you, buddy, except for writing their name in the snow, women can do *everything* you can."

Zee leaned to Wren's ear. "What is snow, and how do men write their name in it?" Wren slapped his chest.

"Don't ask because I'm not explaining it," Wren said. "Let's go and let these two *negotiate*."

Iridia nodded to him. "I am happy to meet you, Ferrus. Hopefully, you will have time later to join us for the last meal of the day. You have our permission to wander the forest with no interference from us for privacy if you so want."

Did he ever want. He glanced at his mate. They needed to talk about more than just the other females. His eyes were opening to a new life.

But could he hold onto it?

CHAPTER EIGHTEEN

Lilah couldn't believe Ferrus was the one to work with her. Maybe he asked to be the go-between. After Zee and Iridia walked away from meeting the red fae, the clan returned to their regular routines.

"Lilah, we need to talk in private, please."

She nodded. "I agree. Let's take a walk. I don't want to be cooped up in a dome of dirt." With his hand in hers, she led him through the village. "Ferrus, see how men and women work together. They talk and laugh and are quite productive." They walked quietly for a moment, then he gasped, and the grip on her hand tightened.

He turned his face to her, shielding his eyes

with his hand. "The females wear no tops. Only long pants."

Lilah snorted. "You just noticed that? Seriously?"

He turned her chin toward him. "I have eyes for only one female. I see no one else."

Her heart jumped into overdrive. No one had ever said anything so romantic to her. Like Iridia said, a mate didn't look at other women. She continued walking to an opening where they stepped into the forest. Her hand was still in his. He hadn't pulled away. He did want to be with her. But first, business.

"Ferrus, you understand why we are striking, don't you?"

"I'm not sure of the word or its purpose. Please explain."

"Striking is not doing what you are expected to do, and using that as a bargaining device. We are not coming back to cook and clean until the king gives us what we want." He stared into the distance. She didn't know if he understood what she said or was pissed because of it. But this was the starting point. Everything else rooted from this.

"Ferrus, it's important for the king to take the

females as equals. As I said earlier, women can do anything men can that doesn't require a ..." Her face heated, realizing what she was about to say and to whom. Sure, she could spout *dick* to the king, but not the guy she wanted to kiss. Geesh, what was wrong with her?

"I understand." He chuckled. "Writing in the snow is a brilliant example for the men to comprehend."

"Not too bright, are they, huh?"

He laughed, pulling her closer as they strolled. "Some are meant to be warriors and nothing else."

"I believe that. Ferrus, I hate to be blunt, but that's the way I am. My job requires it. The men need to suck it up."

"I don't understand, *suck it up.*"

"That means you and the men need to learn to control yourselves like adults do. They need to take responsibility for their actions. They are not children who cry when they don't get their way. They must act like adults, which means they control themselves when around women."

"In the past, it had been...difficult for the men to fight what the body desires." His eyes drilled into her while he spoke. It felt like he was talking from personal experience. She swallowed hard, determined to do this for the women.

"Well, now it's time for them to grow up. If they can't keep themselves from attacking women, then they might as well live in the woods like animals because that's what they are."

"Saying that would enrage the men."

"Then you tell them they must act like fae. Sex won't stop if the men sleep in their own beds. They will only be with a woman who wants to be with them. No more males choosing who they want. Got it?"

"Yes, got it."

"It's unjust that the women are forced to cover themselves because of the men being immature. Self-control needs to be on the man's part too. As I said, grow up and act like an adult. Also, when it comes to meals, the women will continue to cook. We'll deal with that issue later. Will you have enough food until we come back?"

He laughed. "The men do love their steaks. And yes, it would be a good thing to have the females to cook."

"But they won't be serving the men anymore." She put up a hand to stop his rebuttal. "They will prepare and put the food on the tables for the men to fill their plates themselves and pour their own water. Additional tables and chairs should also be made for the women to eat at the same time if they wish."

His eyes widened, and she almost laughed. "Ferrus, these are basic, God-given rights. Men and women should do the same work. It's not fair if they don't, and then jealousy grows. Jealousy leads to anger and hate, then you have a problem on your hands. If everyone is happy, then everything runs smoothly."

"I understand what you are telling me, but women cannot swing a sword to defend their home. Only the men can protect the females."

"I have two things for that. The first is, why do you think hefting a sword is the only way to protect something? The fae in the village use arrows. And, I hate to say it, but arrows are way better than swords. You can kill the enemy before they even get close."

"The second thing?" he asked, not too happy that she was trashing his beliefs.

"The women have knives they use to cut and dice food that are superior to your swords. The small blades can cut through rock without being damaged. Can your swords do that?"

He stopped in his tracks. "How can that be? We have the best weapons. Only our fae can manipulate rock and metal. And the women do not know how to make metal blades."

"Oh, really?" she replied. "I believe a young lady by the name of Muriel creates beautiful hilts and handholds for your swords as well as pours the metal liquid into molds."

"Oh, that is right. She does. She cannot communicate, so Fath—the king put her down there where she did not need to talk with anyone."

Lilah bit down on her lip. "You understand why that pisses me off to no end, right?" He didn't respond. She'd make it clear for him. "She doesn't want to be there. At least full time. You are making her do what she doesn't want and shouldn't have to do without breaks and others to take over occasionally."

"But no one else wants to have that job. It is very hot and strenuous. If we do not make someone do it, it will not get done. Then what?"

"Then you give an incentive, a reward, for doing it. A little good balances out the little bad. If the good is good enough, then someone will do the job."

His brow raised. "Never thought of it that way."

He paused. "How does that explain how the female's knives are better than our swords."

She let out a deep breath. "Ferrus, do the king or the prince ever listen to what a female has to say?"

"Females are not allowed to speak to the king unless given permission."

"Exactly my point. The women have discovered many things that would make your home so much better, but no one will listen to them. So, they help themselves, and you men can do whatever you want. Which is training for battle, not thinking how to advance technology to make your home a better place."

He lifted her hand and rubbed his fingers over the back. "Where are humans from?"

Her mouth opened, then she closed it. Before leaving for the standing stones, she and her cousins had decided not to tell anyone but the Gnoleon about themselves or where they were going. Safety-wise, it was better that no one knew. But she didn't want to lie to Ferrus. She trusted him. Which was sort of dumb since she didn't know him well enough.

"Humans are from a planet called Earth in a different dimension. They are a non-magical species. They can't mold rock or make plants grow faster."

"How do they survive then? They must be very primitive."

She snorted. "You'd think that. The only thing primitive is how they can treat each other."

Lilah glanced up through the high canopy, seeing the sun had moved a distance from where it was when they started walking. Funny how some things didn't change from species to species or planet to planet. The sun here warmed the ground and helped to grow plants. The beings needed water to drink to stay alive and food to fuel the body.

So why humans treated each other differently made no sense. They all shared the same resources, had the same emotions, the same ideas. Why some thought they were above others, she didn't get. Money might get them more things they would never use. More stuff to hang on the wall. More crap to shove into a closet and forget about. But that didn't make them better. It made their homes more cluttered with shit.

Money didn't make one happy. It was the relationship with others that doomed or gifted you. In this case, she had struck it rich.

CHAPTER NINETEEN

Lilah and Ferrus were deep in the woods where the ground cover was thicker, and the trees had changed from black trunks to cream. Strange looking. They'd been talking and sharing for hours though it didn't seem that long. She liked listening to him, just being with him.

Ferrus sat on a fallen log and pulled her down beside him. Close enough that she might as well have been in his lap, which wouldn't be bad. She'd sit on him any time he wanted. Especially when he was naked and on his back.

She couldn't control the shudder that went through her with the thought. Her lower belly twinged, knowing that was a possibility she wanted so badly.

She was about to answer his question of how humans treated each other when he asked another question. "How were *you* treated by others?"

"Me?" She put a hand on her chest. "Why would you want to know that?"

He smiled and looked at his feet. "I want to know everything about you, Lilah, human from planet Earth."

The only time she'd heard *I want to know everything about you* was in sappy movies where the characters were falling in love. That's how she felt about him. She wanted to know everything. What he liked, disliked, his favorite meal, what he did for fun, all of it. But he asked that of her. Did that mean...

She remembered the moment in the mine tunnel when he flattened her against the cave wall. He hadn't touched her, but damn. He couldn't get any closer and not come in contact. The fierce look on his face, the way his body surrounded hers. If she hadn't been so angry at the time, she would've stripped him from his Speedos on the spot. Then she remembered what he told her—*I am never letting you go. Get used to that right now. You are mine.*

"Ferrus," she said in a whisper. He turned to

her. His face was so close to hers. Dare she ask him if he was attracted to her? Could she take the embarrassing rejection when he said no? Could she at least say something, so he didn't think she was an idiot?

He brushed his finger along her jawline. "You are the most beautiful female on this planet. You know that, right?" She shook her head an inch, her eyes locked on his. He was so close, she felt his heat, smelled his snowy scent.

He surrounded her, but she wanted more. His luscious lips, which she wanted to kiss, moved right there. Teasing her. He said, "From the first moment I saw you, I have not been able to stop thinking about you. You have been embedded inside my head. I do not want to be without you."

"Is that what you meant when you said I was yours, and you're never letting me go?"

Ferrus pulled away, the moment gone. He ran his fingers through his hair. "I apologize for scaring you. I was angry and said words..." He stopped, his eyes searching the trees for some answer.

"Did you mean them, or were they only to frighten me, to give you power over me?"

His head whipped toward her. Those eyes were

so intense, so focused on her, she felt the world slip away to just the two of them.

"The only time I want power over you is when I have you in my bed. I want to show you how a warrior makes love to his mate, so he is branded on her heart, in her soul. It will be me you long for when I am not there. It will be me to fill you with my cock until you scream my name. It will be me who takes care of you and protects you from anything that would hurt you."

She couldn't breathe. Her body thumped for him. It wanted to thump him. Oh my god. She believed every word. For once, she wanted to give in to yearning, to feel wanted, loved. For once, she wanted to be treated as someone desirable, someone sexy.

His head dipped to her and kissed her. The first touch of his lips against hers and she moaned at the feeling. Nothing had ever been as perfect as her first kiss with him. Ferrus ran his tongue along the seam of her lips, and she shivered at the touch. She parted her lips to taste him truly, but he was just as eager.

At first, they lightly explored each other's mouths, and her head swam with his scent, his touch, his taste. This was the best kiss she had ever experienced. This was what she had been missing all her life. Genuine passion. No one else had ever given her cause to shake all over from a simple kiss. No one had ever made her feel loved quite like Ferrus with just a simple kiss.

Lilah couldn't help the sadness and anger that shot through her when thinking about how the boys treated her in school. This was so different. This was real.

"You are not smiling. Why not? I will make it better."

She shook her head. "I was just thinking about stupid stuff in my past."

Ferrus suddenly stood with her hand in his and hauled her toward a large tree. He sat with his back against the trunk then pulled her down to sit between his thighs. His arms went around her as she leaned her head back on his chest.

"Here, now I have you safe where nothing bad will happen. Nothing will hurt you, even those memories you do not want to remember. I will protect you from their pain."

Lilah sat there, not believing that someone wanted to listen to the sob story of her life. Nobody, not even best friends, asked for such misery to be cast on them. Did she really want him to know the worst part of her? The most vulnerable moments when she was torn to pieces over simple words?

"I don't think you know what you're asking," she replied.

He pulled her hair to one side and kissed the curve of her neck. "You are right." He paused for a moment, then spoke in a low voice into her ear. "Shortly after my two hundredth peak—"

What did he just say? If she understood correctly, peaks were equivalent to years. But she didn't know how many days were between peaks. But two hundred anything seemed way too many. "How many peaks old are you?"

"I have been alive for a little over five hundred."

Her jaw dropped. She couldn't believe he was that old. "How many peaks do fae live?"

"My father is almost a thousand. My grandfather was fifteen hundred before he went to the spirit."

"Oh, okay then. Sorry I interrupted. What happened when you were so young?" She had a feeling this wasn't going to be a happy story. He was going to share with her the most painful experience he'd had when he was a child. Tears already crept into her eyes, knowing that he had suffered terribly. If she could take away his hurt, she would.

"My mother," he said, "was a wonderful fae. Not only was she beautiful outside, but she was also beautiful inside. She loved everyone she met and let them know how special they were to the world. She would give anything she had to make someone else's life better, whether that be a material item or just a caring word.

"She loved me and spoiled me with her time and affection. I knew I was wanted and loved at all times. Even when I took too much rock from a wall, and it collapsed, crushing everything in my room. That is when I learned moderation was important in life." He laughed.

"My father was so mad at me for that. It took cycles before the adults had put the wall back together. Mother considered it a learning experience while Father saw it as a mess."

His arms tightened around her. "That was the difference between my parents. Mother saw the good in everything while Father saw the worst. So, when Mother became ill after giving birth to my sister, my father expected the worst, which happened. She went to the spirit, leaving us to make do on our own.

"After that, Father was not the same. It seemed that Mother took with her all that was good and light about him. He became withdrawn and was difficult to talk to without angering easily. I learned to stay away from him for the most part. I did my time in the mines and grew to be the strongest and most tireless worker.

"That was, of course, how I got through the transition of my life from doted on child to unwanted, uncared about young adult."

Lilah twisted around in his arms and wiped away the wetness on his cheek. "No, Ferrus, that couldn't have been true. Your father still loved you. He just had trouble showing it."

He chuckled. "We are a warrior race. Showing emotion is not looked upon as favorable."

Lilah rolled her eyes. "Of course, it wasn't. I guess some things are universal. What about your sister?"

"Father spared no expense for her. She was his princess. She was allowed things no others were."

"She was his favorite? I'm so sorry you felt like second place. I know how that feels."

He tilted his head down and kissed the tears on her own cheeks. "Your siblings were more important too?"

She snorted. "Worse. My mother wanted my cousin as a daughter instead of me."

"Mothers love all their children, Lili." He kissed her forehead then turned her around, so she rested her back against him again, snuggling her into him.

Her breath stuck in her throat. Ferrus called her by a nickname, and she loved it. She knew the significance of such a term of endearment. Only those you really cared about had that kind of name. Her mother always called her father "sugar," and Dad called her mother by her middle name, which no one else used.

Did this mean he really cared for her? That he wanted to be with her?

She bent her knees, folding her legs to her chest. She began, "Growing up, my mother always compared me to Daphne."

Ferrus jerked back. "This Daphne? The one with you?" She nodded. "Why would your mother do that? That female is thin with lean muscle and skinny hips. You are perfect, Lili." His hands slid under her knees then dragged the length of her thigh, fingers brushing against the V in her legs. Then up around her hips. "You do not know what you do to me."

She nearly fainted, she was so turned on. So ready for his touch. God, she felt like a teenager "in love." But, like all the times before, would her hopes of finding love be fruitless?

She asked, "How can you like me so much when the boys only called me names like fatty and thunder thighs?"

He suckled on her neck with a tiny bite sending heat straight to her core. "Because boys are children who do not know how to treat the precious things in life. I am a man who knows to treasure what is truly rare and valuable. That is what you are to me, Lili. Someone my heart and body craves."

Yes, this was what she'd been searching for her entire life. Someone who loved her for her. Someone willing to look past her physical flaws to the real person inside. Not the angry, grumpy persona she always wore to hide her vulnerability.

"Lili," he said, "there is a place for everyone. Your entire life, you've been in the wrong place where those there did not accept you. Now, with me, you are home where you belong. Where you will be loved like you deserved to be. You are my mate, Lili. I will love you forever. Only you. I cannot live without you with me."

She turned toward him, and he lifted her, placing her where she straddled his lap, her pussy pressed against his long thick cock. His lips took hers in a hungry kiss. His hands brushed down her back to her ass, where he palmed each side and moaned deep in his throat, rubbing her up and down his length.

Fuck, she wanted this. Needed this. The two guys she'd had sex with in college did nothing for her. One was drunk, the other insisted the lights be off so he wouldn't see her. Yeah, that hurt. But this made up for it. She would take Ferrus as her mate. Everyone else could fuck off. The prince would just have to get along without her.

She'd chosen someone she could love with all her heart and not be afraid of him leaving her or becoming disgusted with her.

Her man. Her mate.

CHAPTER TWENTY

Lilah was making out with the man of her dreams. The man who would love her and never let her down. He was sexy, strong, smart, and from what she could feel, a dick big enough to send her over the edge quickly.

Ferrus moved a hand off her body, instantly leaving a cold spot she wanted warmed again. She didn't know how he did it, but he rolled her onto a soft, cushy surface. Thinking it was the dirty ground with bugs and shit, she pushed him up away from lying on her.

"Wait. We can't—" Seeing a stone-colored mat underneath them, she was speechless. Where had that come from? And how in the hell was it as soft as a mattress?

Ferrus's brow raised. "Guess you have not seen one of our sleeping caves."

"No. I haven't. How did you make this? The ground is soil."

"Even a forest dirt floor has some type of rock mixed in with it. I called it up and made it into a solid piece but kept it pliable so it would mold to our bodies, making my loving you so much better."

"Oh, that's how you sleep? On a soft spot of rock?"

He lay over her again. "Yes. Let me show you how comfortable it is."

Lilah laid back and was pleasantly surprised to find the rock was comfortable, but her attention was drawn to the man in front of her. She wanted to feel his body on hers, and she didn't care if the rock was pliable right then.

She leaned into his face and gave him her lips. She'd been dying for another taste of him. Her body flamed inside. He took her lips like he owned them. She dug her nails into his

chest and pulled him down next to her body. His smooth skin made her yearn for more contact.

His hand slid down her waist to her pants, slipped into her panties, and spread her pussy lips, zeroing in on her clit. Lilah moaned and clutched at the dirt and stone mat they lay on. Ferrus slipped his hand from her panties, gliding up to her bra, and freeing her of the garment. He cupped her plump breasts and tweaked her nipples, and she moaned.

Her pulse thrummed wild in her ears. Ferrus pulled on her panties at the same time he licked his way down her chest.

Lilah ran her hands down his chest to the material that covered his cock. She wanted to touch him and see him. She bit her lip and reached for him. So smooth and hot. Her gaze jerked to his face when she heard him groan.

"Your skin on me feels great," Ferrus said, curling a hand around hers. He kissed her again. Every time he did, it was as if he could not get enough of her taste. He groaned and thrust his hips into her.

Lilah wanted nothing between them but skin, she spread her legs farther. He leaned forward, sucking one of her breasts into his mouth and running his finger through her lips. One finger slid into her. Then another. Soon he was fucking her deep and fast while moving from one nipple to the other, stopping at the valley of her breasts to lick up and down her chest.

She clung to Ferrus's hair, holding him close to her body. His lips moved closer, licking a circle around her clit and sending fire shooting down her back. He groaned, drove his tongue into her channel, and pressed his face into her pussy. His nose rubbed against her clit perfectly while he fucked her with his tongue hard enough to make her whimper.

Her muscles tightened with her oncoming orgasm. Ferrus moved his licking to go from her entrance up to her clit and back down. Electricity exploded through her system, leaving her screaming and shaking. With every breath, a new wave of delight journeyed through her blood.

Ferrus pushed the head of his cock into her pussy. She curled her legs around his hips.

He drove deep, slamming his cock into her.

Tension coiled at the pit of her stomach. With every drive, Ferrus pushed her closer to the edge of pleasure. In. Out. Hard. Fast. Ferrus didn't let up. She choked on her breaths, her lungs tripping over themselves, trying to get a breath.

Ferrus slammed his hips into her pussy, finally sending her flying with her earth-shattering release. She screamed. What? Something unintelligible, but she screamed. Her pussy tightened around his cock, sucking him deeply.

One final thrust and he came inside her. Lilah drifted off to sleep, with a smile on her face. Content for the first time in her life, knowing she was safe.

CHAPTER TWENTY-ONE

When Lilah woke, the sunlight sat low in the sky, and she lay in the arms of heaven. She had spent all day with her Prince Charming and fell in love with him. He called her mate, and Lilah believed him with her whole heart. Just thinking she had what Wren and all the others in the village had, she was giddy with happiness. A forever kind of love with a fantastic tongue and magic cock.

Ever so softly, his hand brushed along her waist, tickling her. She wiggled against him, trying not to giggle, her naked body pressing against his. His eyes opened.

"I liked that little move. Do it again." The spark

in his eye set a flame low in her stomach. Could she handle another round of orgasms? Hell yes!

"You're tickling me. I'm totally in your hands to do as you please."

When his smile dimmed, she worried. "What?"

"I am not tickling you."

She felt his hand brush across her lower back, sending chills down her legs. "Yes, you are."

When he sat up, she raised her upper body, and his hand slid all the way around her, which was impossible. It tightened, squeezing the breath out of her, then she was yanked away. She screamed from surprise, realizing it wasn't Ferrus who was touching her.

She hit the ground but kept moving. Something was dragging her, fast. She glanced at Ferrus and saw terror in his eyes. Her hands grabbed onto whatever was around her waist. It was thick like an inner tube in the pool and felt like steel with a leathery covering. Perplexed what kind of "rope" had her, she tried to push it off, but it didn't budge.

Ferrus screamed her name and ran toward her. Then she was jerked straight up into the air and thrashed about, but the rope held her tightly. When her head smacked a tree limb, she realized she was being hauled up a tree. What the fuck was going on?

She was finally turned in a direction where she could see where the line around her originated. It wasn't a rope but a thirty-foot-long fucking python. A scream tore from her lungs, scratching up her throat. Her body whipped through the air as the snake slithered from one tree branch to another, trying to escape with its meal. That thought brought another scream for her.

She pounded and beat on the solid muscle around her, but all it did was tighten more. Her lungs crushed in, and she fought for breath. Somewhere behind her and her captor, she heard a herd of elephants tromping toward them. The only thing she could hope for was for them to stomp the snake to death. But being in a tree, that wasn't going to happen.

Lilah hung midair as the rest of the snake wrapped its dark body around a thick limb. Its head slithered around to her; eyes fixed on hers. Not one, but two tongues slipped out and flipped at her. She would've screamed again, but the bands constricted her chest too. She was going to die from asphyxiation, squeezed to death by a giant snake.

The snake opened its mouth wide enough to swallow a cow whole, not to mention the foot-long fangs that dripped with a liquid. A dark weapon of some kind swung up from the ground, slamming into the bottom jaw, knocking the mouth closed and the head back. Another set of dark ropes wrapped around her. Again, not hemp rope, but something else. Something alive.

The python didn't let her go. Her body stretched in a tug of war that only she would lose as each creature made away with half of her. Then the silverish black arm of the second creature reached forward and grabbed the serpent behind its head. The snake thrashed about, and she got her first look at the second beast.

Again, she would've screamed if she had the breath. The animal was a cross between Godzilla and a T-Rex, standing thirty feet tall. She'd seen this being on the doors to the throne room.

Adrenaline raced through her with hope. "Ferrus?" she breathed. The dragon's eyes darted to her, distracting him. The python stretched its head forward and tried to sink its fangs in Ferrus's dragon arm. But instead of slicing through flesh, the teeth clanged against a hard-outer shell. She wasn't sure, but she thought she saw the point of one of the fangs chip off. Ha. That's what it deserved.

The steel bands around her loosened, and she sucked in a deep breath. Ferrus pulled her away and then leaned forward in the snake's face and let out a stream of molten lava just like the magma river down where they melted rock to make swords.

Wait. Was that what covered the dragon's body, skin made of metal? It would make as much sense as anything else in this world from hell.

Adrenaline and being scared shitless drained her strength immediately. Her body went limp, and her vision tunneled down to darkness.

When she opened her eyes, she didn't know where she was. The space was mostly dark, with light coming from the ground. The smell of fresh soil was familiar.

"Lili?" She heard her lover's voice low in her ear. He was here, wrapped around her. She knew she was protected and relaxed the growing panic in her.

"Ferrus," she whispered. He kissed her neck.

"I am here, love. The tree fae built us a dome to sleep in. You are safe with me."

She lay her head on the soft ground they were

on. "What happened? I remember a dragon puking lava on the head of a monster python."

His body shook lightly as he chuckled against her back in their spoon position. "You recall correctly."

"Was that you?"

"Yes," he replied, hesitancy in his voice.

"You're incredibly amazing, Ferrus. Your dragon is stunning to see."

"You are not afraid of me?"

"Of course not. I know you won't hurt me in that form. I mean, Zee didn't eat any of us in his scary-as-shit cat form."

"The forest alpha is a changeling also?"

"Yes," she said. "Maybe keep that to yourself. I probably wasn't supposed to let that secret out."

"No worries, my love. Rest now. The sun won't be up for a while yet. I'll protect you until the village awakens, and it is time for me to return to the king."

She rolled over in his arms. Her fingers glided over the side of his strong jaw and high cheek-bones. "You're coming back, right?"

"You could not keep me away." He leaned in and kissed her. Lilah moaned as he brushed his tongue against hers. She couldn't believe how lucky she was to find him. Ferrus leaned back and peppered kisses across her cheek, then down her neck.

"You are tempting me, mate. It is a good thing we have time before I must depart." Ferrus grinned, and then ran his hand up her thigh, across her stomach, and stopped with his hand cupping her breast. With the chills rushing along her flesh, she realized she was naked.

He glanced down at her breast, and she bit her lip. She wanted to feel his mouth on her skin again. She wanted to feel him on her body. Lilah ran her hands up his arms and around his neck, then back down his arms. "Ferrus, let me explore your body, please."

Lilah chuckled as her words caused his body to shudder, and his hooded gaze burned brighter. He nodded and dropped onto his back next to her and placed his hands behind his head, watching her.

She giggled and sat up next to him. She paused for a moment, debating what her next move would be. Finally, she slung her leg over his hips and straddled him. She could feel his hard cock nestled against her body and froze in place for a moment.

Lilah leaned down and placed kisses on his chest, from his neck down to his stomach. Each kiss caused his muscles to contract, and his breathing turned shallow. Lilah kept scooting her body down his legs and dropping a kiss with each inch she uncovered.

She ran her hands across his thighs and grasped his cock tightly in her fist. Slowly she swiped her thumb across his tip and licked her lips at the precum. Ferrus dropped his head to the ground with a loud moan.

Lilah grinned and moved her hand down his shaft, then with a tighter grip, she moved her hand up his hard length. With each movement of her hand, his hips lifted off the ground. She loved the power she had over his body. She alternated squeezing and twisting her hand around his cock. She slowly lowered her head and licked his tip and groaned at the taste flooding her mouth.

Lilah moved her hand down to the base of his cock and sank her mouth around his length. She moaned and sucked as she lifted her mouth, swirling her tongue on the tip as she reached it. Ferrus threaded his fingers through her hair and tugged lightly, the motion caused her pussy to throb.

Lilah ran her free hand down to her clit and rubbed it.

"No, that is mine to play with, mate. Flip around and let me taste you." Ferrus growled, and Lilah couldn't move fast enough. She wanted to feel his tongue on her pussy again. Last night was outstanding, and she wanted to feel it again.

With a pop of her lips, she lifted her mouth from his cock and pushed up into a sitting position, then swung her leg over him. For a second, she debated the smoothest way to get into position. Would her stomach and thighs make it hard for him to reach her pussy. Maybe it wasn't a good idea. She didn't want to smother him with her thunder thighs after all.

"I can see the wheels turning in your head, stop thinking. Put your pussy above my face and let me eat my meal. I can't wait to feast on you again. Nothing will stop me, mate." Ferrus tugged on her hand to get her moving, and she relented.

"This has to be the most unattractive position to have sex in, Ferrus." Lilah chuckled but only for a moment. Ferrus lifted his hips, and his cock was so close to her mouth.

She licked the tip, just as he licked her, starting at her ass and going down to her clit. Lilah moaned, and Ferrus's hands clenched on her thighs. She moaned again and felt his hips lifting.

Ferrus licked her faster, swirling his tongue around her clit. Lilah's breath came in quick pants as she tried to focus on his cock. Not what he was doing with his very talented tongue.

She squeezed his cock at the base and took him as deep as she could, then hummed as she lifted her head slightly. His hands tightened on her legs, and she laughed lightly. She swirled her tongue on his head and took him deep again. Ferrus groaned and started licking her faster, moving one of his fingers into her pussy and fucking her with it.

His cum, shot down her throat, and she eagerly swallowed every bit. Humming to help finish him off as he brought her to an orgasm. She screamed and hoped the dirt mound they were in was soundproof.

CHAPTER TWENTY-TWO

The next morning, with his mate securely in his life, Ferrus headed back to the cave to convince the king times have changed as well as his people. The females were completely correct in wanting what they did, fairness and equality. But how was he going to convince his father of that?

Close to the edge of the forest, his dragon picked up something that set it on alert. He stopped and sniffed the air. Pine, bark, and dirt were the only scents he took in. Normal. With his animal's eyes peeking through, he scanned the area for movement; his ears listened for heartbeats.

Only the tiny rodents and insects of the trees and ground rummage around. Nothing to indicate fear on their part. Finding no reason for further searching, returned on his way home.

When he approached the main cave entrance, his men came from their hiding places to greet him. The first thing he noticed was how uncomfortable they both looked. They stood at attention, but one's bottoms were about to slide off his hips while the other looked like he couldn't suck his stomach in more and breathe, the latch on the waistband about to burst.

Strange, but if that was how they wanted to clothe themselves, then fine with him as long as they fought like warriors.

"How are the soldiers holding up without the females?" he asked. The two guards glanced at each other with frowns then turned back to him. "What?" They were not telling him something.

"Sire, the king awaits your return."

He continued past them into the main cavern. The area was quieter than expected. No one was training or moving about. Where were his men? The only other place that could hold them was the eating room.

He hurried up the tunnel toward the crest of the mountain. When he reached the top, he heard voices and entered the cave to see dishes in upheaval around the tables, most with little food remaining. The floor was dotted with spilled items. It looked like a herd of animals had grazed in the room. Not to mention the smell.

Leaving, he strode down the hall to the food prep room where most of the noise was coming from. As soon as his eyes adjusted to the sunlight, he wished he had remained blind to the sight. The place was a disaster.

Bowls were piled everywhere, several smashed on the floor. Greens and skins littered the stone. A few men stood at the central stone section carving a head out of a melon. He could see shadows of the men outside doing who knew what. Some were partially dressed, and others had on clothes too big or too small. To top it off, three men lounged in the pool.

The females were going to kill them...after they put the room back in order.

"Glad you're here, sire. When are the females coming back? We don't know how to make porridge. We're out of meat since some of the men *had* to have another steak. And we're not sure what some items in the garden are."

Ferrus stepped backward then continued down the aisle to the tunnel that went past the throne room. He didn't even know where to start with all that.

"Sire," he heard, "are you coming back? We're hungry." They'd figure out the answer when he didn't show up.

From a connecting tunnel, Smit stepped out with several swords in his arms. Very rough looking swords. "Morning, sire. I'm taking these weapons to the men to inspect." Ferrus lifted one, a sharp edge pressed into his hand. "You'll have to forgive me, sire. I cannot make the handholds that the female does. We need her back."

"You *need* her back?" he asked, brow raised.

"Yes, sire. No one can do that job but her."

Ferrus nodded. "I will see what I can do. Take these to the men and tell them what you just told me. I want them to see how *they* need the females also." Smit bowed his head and continued up the tunnel.

Entering the throne room, Ferrus heard more yelling and dishes breaking. The king stood outside his private area, throwing yesterday's breakfast items to the floor.

"Father?" he asked.

"Flame focker," the king cursed, "get those females back here at once, Ferrus. I have not eaten since yesterday. And I cannot wear my robes until a stain is washed out."

Ferrus smiled. "Seems you need the females as well, Father." The coldness in the king's eyes sent a chill down him. He was the king for a reason.

"I expected you back last night, son. Good to see the females have not persuaded you to their side."

There really was not much persuading needed. He saw what was fair and how they all had to work together as a large team to make a successful clan survive like the Gnoleon. He wondered how he should approach this. Demon's hell, Ferra knew how to do this kind of thing better than he did.

He was a fighter. He did not have a smooth tongue. Good thing for his mate since she enjoyed his tongue quite a bit. The image of her writhing under his assault on her pussy flashed in his mind. Dragon balls, he was getting hard. That was the last thing he wanted his father to see.

Calming himself, he continued into the room. "Father," he said, "do you understand why the females are on strike."

The king slammed a lid on the cart, shattering the dish. "I do not even know what the damnation word means." His father stomped away from the cart to sit hard on his throne.

"It means they are trying to show you how important they are to this clan."

"Important?" his father questioned. Ferrus watched as the king's expression turned darker than ever before. His fist beat on the seat's arm. "Is that what they want? To be important?"

"No, Father. They know they are needed. You just need to admit it. They want the right to choose whether they sleep alone or with a male."

His father's brow raised. "If the males do not have a release, it will distract them from their fighting."

"I learned a new saying. The men need to 'suck it up' and grow up. They are not children who cannot control themselves. They must abide by the female's wishes. Even in nature, the female sometimes decides which mate she will take."

His father grumbled, crossing his arms over his chest. "Anything else?"

Ferrus chuckled. "There is a list, sire."

The king's mouth dropped open, his eyes widening. "What more could they want?"

"They do not want to be forced to wear the brown coverups."

"But the males will—"

"Sire, that is another one of those 'grow up' items. They can and will control and restrain. They will continue feeding us as long as they no longer have to serve the men at the tables. They will bring the food to the room, but the men will fill their own cups and plates."

His father's breathing came faster and shallower. Ferrus had not even gotten to the most critical demand. Should he list it or let it be? His mate was so set on mates working together. It worked well for the forest fae. Why couldn't they do the same? Besides, he wasn't about to not have his mate beside him.

"One more thing. They want mates to be acceptable."

The king rose from his throne, holding his arm out. "NEVER." He stamped into his rooms and slammed the rock walls together to close off access, knocking loose a shower of pebbles.

Clapping came from the tunnel entrance. Silvo stepped in with a saunter, a sneering smile on his face. "Wonderful presentation, Ferrus." Occasionally, in a personal setting, he'll let his men call him by his name. But only in closed quarters.

"You will honor me as our rules command, or I will kill you."

Silvo snapped his arms up in a surrender fashion while bending at the waist. "Forgive me, *sire*. I forget myself." He returned to his upright stance, the haughtiness still showing. "Seems His Majesty is not happy with the female demands. And, rightly, he shouldn't be."

"Why is that, Silvo?" Ferrus looked at him with disdain. The man thought he had more power than he did. Just because Silvo was in charge when Ferrus was gone did not mean the ass was on the same level. Perhaps the subordinate needed a reminder.

"Why?" Silvo replied, taking a step toward him. "A female's only purpose is to serve her master in all ways. Males are stronger and should beat his female into submission. That is the way it has always been in most clans, as it should be."

Ferrus stepped up to his second-in-command, noses almost touching. "Let me get this right. Because your bicep is stronger than a female's, you have the right to make her do what you want."

"Yes," Silvo growled.

"Then, by default, since I am stronger than you,

I can make you do what I want. And if you do not, I can beat you for it."

Silvo's eyes narrowed, but he said nothing. His face flooded redder, and he shook with his anger. Ferrus should laugh in his face, but this was a serious matter to him. His mate made him see why he should care.

"And what if one night," Ferrus continued, "while you are sleeping, she decides she's had enough of you. How easy would it be for her to take a prep knife and do a little *slice, slice*?" With his hands, he made a small slashing gesture. "Bye-bye balls." Ferrus turned his back to him to see where his father had gone to.

Before he made it a few steps away, his animal cried danger, and instincts had him spinning on his foot to catch a flying food prep knife that would have pierced his heart through the back.

"Ah, thank you for the weapon, Silvo," Ferrus said. "Now go before I *slice, slice*." Silvo left the room as slowly as he could to prove to Ferrus he was not afraid. Nice try. Ferrus saw the fear in the male's eye.

The entrance to the king's rooms slid open. "Silvo, stay," the King commanded as he stepped out. "Ferrus, I have changed my mind. Bring the females back, and I will be pleased to talk. Tell them to bring food so we can eat."

An empty stomach was a good negotiator. "Yes, sire. We will return around the midday meal with food."

Ferrus hurried out the front entrance, eager to see his mate again. There was hope for a happy, peaceful resolution that would advance his people.

He wondered why his father had Silvo stay. Probably to admonish the ass for throwing a knife toward Ferrus.

CHAPTER TWENTY-THREE

After breakfast was finished and everything was cleaned, both brown and red fae mixed throughout the village, talking and learning new ways from each other.

Lilah sat with her cousins, the alphas, and the elders in the middle of the village. After warning them about the monster snake, she outlined her ideas from talking with Ferrus yesterday. She asked for input from those who had been alive much longer than she had.

The older woman Lilah knew as the Storyteller from their time with the Gnoleon, shook her head. "In the past, those who have wandered far and returned to us have told us about the red fae. They are a warrior species. Fighting is ingrained in their blood, no compromise. I would be cautious, young one."

"But you met Ferrus," Lilah said in reply. "Don't you think he's not that way? That he sees both sides?"

Daphne added, "He's definitely not like the rest of the men. Especially one in particular who likes to slap women around."

Lilah thought back to the time in the dining room where the asshole hit the lady pouring his water. That shit would absolutely be coming to a stop. "He's got the personality of the king. Arrogant and a prick."

The elders glanced at each other. One asked, "We are unfamiliar with the word *prick*."

Lilah's face flooded hot, and her cousins laughed. She didn't know what to say. She wasn't about to talk about cocks in front of what amounted to be grandparents. Daph came to her rescue. "In this case, it means he's not a good person."

Zee jumped to his feet, staring into the forest. "Someone approaches." After a few moments, one of the village guards came into sight with Ferrus beside him.

Lilah hopped up, excited that he was back. She was waiting for him and the guard to reach them, but she found herself walking, then running toward him. She was too damn happy to be patient. Hell, she was almost giggling. When was the last time she'd done that? Like when she was twelve?

The smile on his gorgeous face told her he was just as happy to see her. Was this real? After having sex so soon, she was sure he'd never come back. That he'd leave because he couldn't stand the sight of her. But he was here. Her heart exploded with emotions she had never let herself experience. He. Was. Hers.

To hide her sudden tears, she threw her arms around his neck, not caring about PDA. The villagers were used to that. His arms went around her tightly, squeezing her entirely against him. It was like he couldn't get close enough.

She felt safe in his arms like nothing in the world would ever hurt her again. Not the haughty looks of skinny women, or the disgusted expression of a boy not wanting to touch her, or those TV commercials that guilt you into being someone you weren't.

He wanted her just the way she was.

He peppered kisses on her face. "I missed you."

She giggled out loud. "You were only gone a few hours."

"A few hours too long." He pulled back and saw droplets on her face. His smile faded. "What is wrong? Did somebody hurt you?" His face started to darken as he kissed her tears.

"No," she breathed out, losing more control over the rock wall around her heart every second. "I'm fine. It's just...I've never been this happy. I've never allowed myself to reach this point. To let go. To make myself so vulnerable to someone. My job demands that nothing affects me, or I would've failed a long time ago. I have to learn how to live like this."

"Yes, you do," he replied with a playfully stern face, "because I am not letting you out of my life. You better get used to all this happiness 'cause I'm going to cram it down your throat." A wicked smile graced his expression, and he leaned closer. "Then, I am going to cram my cock into you until you are screaming my name, begging me to let you come."

Oh my freaking god. A shudder ran through her. No one had ever said anything like that to her in her life. Her undies had never been so wet. Shit, all her girl parts tingled. All she could do was stare at him and lick her lips, thinking about how he would taste in her mouth.

He laughed. "That is much better. My dragon likes what he smells almost as much as I do." He leaned in and kissed her neck. "Is our little dome still up."

"Hey," Wren called from the group of elders, "I know what you're both thinking, and no, it'll have to wait. Get over here." Lilah's face flushed hot enough to make sweat beads pop out on her forehead.

He chuckled, taking her hand. Damn, she was just a blob of goo ready to spread herself all over her man. *Her* man.

Ferrus guided her toward the others as she tried to get her mind straight on what she should be thinking about, which was not how his dick filled her completely, stretching her to such pleasurable pain. Her mate breathed deeply, squeezed her hand, and growled.

He whispered, "You keep thinking what you are thinking, and I am going to throw you over my shoulder, and dirt hut or not, you are going to come harder than you ever have before."

How the hell did he expect her to think about

anything else after saying that? Shit, shit, shit. Snap out of it. After her own deep breath, she pulled it together, but let him wait. There would be a time when turnabout was fair play. And she couldn't wait till that opportunity showed itself.

"Ferrus, what did the king say?" Daphne asked. Her mate sobered quickly, all fun and games over with.

After a moment, he said, "He is willing to negotiate. He is starving."

Her cousins whooped at the seeming victory, but she wasn't all that happy. "Lilah," Daph said, "you have that face that says you're going to chew someone's head off? Isn't this a win?"

Her eyes narrowed as she stared off into the trees. "No, it's not a win. The king gave in way too easily. He doesn't fully understand this isn't a negotiation. It's all or nothing."

Ferrus turned her to him. "I do not understand."

"Negotiating is a give and take. A compromise. How can I tell the women they don't have to wear those ugly ass coverups, but they'll still be forced into sex with whatever man comes to their room at night? No," she shook her head, "I can't do that."

The group was deathly silent. Maybe the

mention of the sexual abuse was too personal to share with the group, but dammit, she refused to let that continue. She'd stay here and fight as long as it took to free these women.

The Storyteller glowered at Ferrus, her eyes flashing a starburst white. "Your king allows this?" She thumped her staff on the ground and twisted it into the dirt. "We will put a stop to this if that means we wipe out the male mountain fae. We defeated the qhasant thousands of cold moons ago. We will defeat the warrior race as well."

In a heartbeat, Ferrus went from sitting to taking a knee with his head bent. "Elders of the Gnoleon fae. My mate speaks the truth, but it is not as it seems. Most of the males share a bed with only their chosen mates. Such couplings are uncontested."

"But you don't allow mates," Lilah replied. But it was good to know most women weren't forced into sex with different men. The elders grumbled among themselves. Shit, she needed to keep her mouth shut before she started a war.

Still on his knee, Ferrus sighed. "The king is unaware of the nightly ritual of mates being together. The…prince, his son, pretends he does not know such a thing happens."

Lilah crossed her arms over her chest. "This prince asshole actually has a heart? I wouldn't have guessed that."

Turning his head slightly, Ferrus gave her a strange look she didn't know how to read.

"You may rise, Ferrus. Your words have saved the lives of the red fae. As has your prince's actions. But there are still those who do not have mates. Is their situation as described?"

He lowered his chin to his chest. "Most of the unmated have paired up with a male of their choosing."

"So are any females forced into such abhorrent slavery?"

A few whispered on the air from him. The look on his tortured face broke Lilah's heart.

"What about the children? Do they sleep in the same room as the adults?" An elder Lilah had never heard speak asked something she hadn't even thought of in the whole scheme of things. What about the children?

"The children sleep together in a deeper section of the cave for their protection. The males have a room to themselves as do the females."

Thank god for small miracles. Despite that good news, her mate was crushed. This law affected him deeply. He was ashamed of it, but what could he do to stop it? The asshole prince would have him killed for insubordination. She laid her hand on his arm.

"Ferrus, there will be no more of this injustice. That will not be a negotiable item. I will break off talks if that's the case."

One of the elders cleared his throat. "The mountain fae females are welcome to stay as long as needed. They seem to get along quite well with us." Looking over her shoulder, Lilah saw a fusion of brown and red beings going about their day as if long-time friends and neighbors.

Despite the difference in skin color, both groups were fae. They all breathed the same air. They all ate from the bounty of the same soil. They all needed love and freedom in their lives. The fundamental God-given rights every living creature deserved. That was what Lilah fought for.

Now, she just had to convince a hard-headed king to give up his fisted control and power over his females. Like it was going to happen that easily.

CHAPTER TWENTY-FOUR

Shame and guilt burned a hole into Ferrus's soul.

He knew the rules the king had in place were unjust, but the men seemed to work things out among themselves. There had been few disagreements that he knew of. But, of course, he tried to stay as far away as possible from all that. He trusted his warriors, and the females were not complaining. Well, until now.

When he became king, all this would stop. But his father wasn't too old. He wasn't nearly close to the end of his life span. This couldn't wait.

His mate stood and brushed her hands over the back of her pants. "I'm ready. Let's go."

"Go where?"

i

Her brows drew down. "Where do you think? I have to *negotiate* with the king." Alarm zipped through him. His dragon did not like that idea. Then her eyes narrowed, and her full lips pressed together. "Don't you even *think* about telling me I can't do this. I do this kinda thing every day, and I'm damn good at it. I'm the only one who can do it."

Demon's hell! There was no way he was changing her mind on this. He knew her well enough to figure that out.

He stood and took her hand. "Can we talk, alone?"

She spun around and yanked him away from the village. Dragon balls, she was angry. Even though she was adorable with the heightened pink in her face, not to mention that as she dragged him forward, he got a great look at her ass, he didn't want his mate upset.

She stopped and turned to him, arms crossing under her plump breasts, lifting them, ready to suck on. What was it about this woman that narrowed his mind to one path? No one had ever enticed him like she did.

"Up here, mate," She pointed to her face. Yes, her beautiful face. He clasped her lips with his and backed her against a tree. He pressed his body against her softness. Every part of her welcomed him. His hand slid down her hip to the back of her thigh, lifting her leg to his waist. The other leg copied the motioned then her ankles were crossed on his back.

His hard cock rubbed over her heat; she was so hot, she radiated through both their garments, keeping him from being buried in her. He could remedy that with a few rips.

"Ferrus," his mate mumbled, "you're not changing my mind about this, no matter how much I want to have you right now."

Damnation. That wasn't his intention, but that proved how dedicated she was to her beliefs. She stood to defend those who couldn't. No one would make her back down. He was so proud of her. She would be a worthy queen of a warrior race.

He let her feet touch the ground. "You are right. I am sorry. I didn't mean to distract you. I need to learn to control myself." *Control himself.* How many times had his mate said his men had to learn self-control? He never thought himself a part of that group. He had always considered himself above all the physical and mental needs.

Now he understood why his men risked so

much to meet their mates in a dark corner or a secluded tunnel. Why it was so hard to wait until the sun disappeared to go to their mates. How could he have been so wrong? His father. The grieving king had taught his son that love wasn't important and even wrong.

"Ferrus?" his mate said in an unsure way. "You okay?"

He chuckled. "I am happy, love. You have changed my life and made me see things I had chosen to ignore. I am ready to talk with the king. I will be with you the entire way." With new understanding and conviction, he would stand by his mate for equality and fairness for all. "Let's gather the females and go home." He took her hand, but she pulled back.

"Wait, we can't all go yet. We haven't started talks."

He didn't understand. His mate's ways would take a while to learn. "But the king has agreed to talk while eating."

"He's *agreed*, Ferrus. That doesn't mean he'll give us all we want. We have to hold out till everything is settled."

"All will be settled shortly afterward, my mate. There is no reason to stay here any longer. Besides, the king and my men are starving. It seems they ate everything they could yesterday and now don't know what to do."

Lilah rolled her eyes. "Of course, they did." She stood a moment, studying the ground. "Do you trust your king will be in good faith about all this? I mean, if we go back and he refuses to budge, we'll have to leave again."

He had to be honest with her. Lying would not ever come in between his mate and him. "He may balk at the mates being together, but that issue is minor since mates are together all night. During the day, everyone is working and apart." But he knew by watching the tree fae that being separated wasn't necessary or even ideal.

"I guess that's something we can work on after we get the bigger things worked out."

After a short meeting with the elders and her cousins—where it was decided Daph and Wren with Zee would remain in the village—the females collected bags of food. Ferrus escorted his mate and the others along the path toward his people and a place that no longer felt like home. On the walk there, his mate was quiet. She was lost in her mind as she thought over her plan. He didn't want to break her concentration.

As they approached the main entrance, something felt wrong. Only one of the guards was in their normal positions overlooking the mountainside. In the short time he'd been gone, had the men gone completely lax to the point of disregarding the clan's safety. This was unacceptable. Where was Silvo? He was to take over while he was gone.

Ferrus guided his mate into the main cavern that looked deserted.

"Where is everyone?" she asked.

"This morning, they were all in the food preparation area, some in the pool."

"What pool?" she asked. "There's only a place to wash clothes and hang them to dry."

Well, that explained that, he thought. Still, something did not sit right with him. The females came in behind them and headed toward the tunnels that led toward the top.

"Valori," Ferrus called out, "the males fed themselves yesterday."

Her eyes grew wide. "Is the room demolished?"

"Sorry." A sheepish grin lined his face.

His mate pulled away from him. "Ferrus, let me go with the women, and I'll bring a tray of food for the king before we sit down. It'll be my peace offering to him."

His grin grew. "You seem to know what you are doing."

"Are you kidding?" she replied. "This isn't my first rodeo." His mate filtered in with the women and was gone. He felt lonely already. He also wondered what a *rodeo* was.

He dragged his feet to the throne room. A dread inside him refused to go away. He trusted his mate, but this meant so much to her. What if something went wrong?

The guard outside the throne room bowed his head. "The king is expecting you, Your Highness." He then opened one of the walls for him to enter. Behind him, the guard said, "He asked that you wait for him to return from his rooms." The wall closed with an echoing *thunk*. He had not noticed that before. Was that an omen?

CHAPTER TWENTY-FIVE

As Lilah walked with the women up the tunnel toward the kitchen, her stomach churned. Sure, she might have done this several times, but that didn't make it any easier. Things could always go wrong. A hand touched her shoulder.

"Lilah," one of the women said. She looked over her shoulder to see a face she recognized but didn't know the lady's name. "All the females want me to tell you that they very much appreciate all you are doing for us. Out of fear, none would risk the security of our home to voice our thoughts to the king or the prince."

"While with the tree fae, we learned and saw many things that pleased us. We wish to live like they do in freedom and happiness. We are certain that you will find a way. We fully put our trust in the alpha female."

Lilah fought back her tears. "I'll do my best." Now she was so nervous about failing that she wanted to throw up. This was the most important "case" she'd ever had. These ladies' futures, and the future generations, depended on the outcome. She stepped to the side and put her back to the cold stone wall and let the others pass. She had to gather herself before going on.

As the women went by, they bowed their heads and mumbled something. *Alpha female*, she thought they were saying. The alpha female was the mate to the prince. She couldn't be the real alpha leader. That meant she had to mate the prince. And Silvo was a complete ass.

Never would she be with that bastard. After dealing with the king, she and Ferrus might have to leave immediately before someone told Silvo about her. Valori had told the women not to tell anyone, but it would have to come out sometime now that they were all back.

She joined the back of the line to continue the trudge up the slope. When she turned down the aisle that passed the kitchen into the dining room, the king and the prince came out of the men's tunnel. What were they doing here? Wait, of course, they were hungry.

Silvo growled at her, and she flashed him a smile just to piss him off. Which worked, if his balled-up hands and darker complexion meant anything.

When the old ruler reached the far side of the wide kitchen entrance, he put his hand on the wall and dragged it like he was closing a curtain on a rod. The wide opening narrowed to a single-person walk-through with him blocking it. And she hadn't gotten inside yet.

Not wanting to be in the hall with only Silvo, she sidled up to the king in the doorway and tried to wedge herself in front of him to slip inside. It didn't work as she hoped.

The king grabbed her arm and held her there. His voice must've boomed in the closed-in kitchen as it was loud out here. He was not happy in the slightest as he told the women they would remain there until he released them.

"Hey," she said, "that's not how this works." She smacked at his grasp on her. The king slammed the doorway closed and ran his hand down the barely-there crevice, sealing it to look like one solid piece of rock. "Are you locking them in there? You can't do that." Now she was pissed. "Look, ass—"

The king stepped away from the wall and threw her toward Silvo. "Here," the old royal said, "I do not want to see her again."

"Yes, sire." The asshat's smile turned evil.

Lilah fought his hold. "What is going on? Ferrus said you wanted to talk."

The wrinkly prick turned to her. "Not with you." He slowly came toward her. "I will talk to the men when I tell them they will no longer be sleeping with their mates." Her jaw dropped. How did he know? "At least one warrior is loyal to his king even if the prince is not." His eyes glanced at Silvo. Some dickhead told the king about the mates? Shit.

Now in her face, the king's spittle landed on her cheek. "And if the females do not like their current wardrobe, they definitely will not like the extra-heavy neck shackles they will wear all day and night."

Lilah's face scrunched. "Hell has a special place for people like you."

"I can thank the new army leader for the idea. He has several forms of punishment that will teach the females what happens when they disobey. And he will make sure you will never marry my son."

She was so furious, she couldn't think of anything evil enough to call him. Instead, she snapped her knee up and smashed his balls. Human or fae, all males had one thing in common. The old man doubled over, his red tone turning grayish.

Silvo jerked her to the side where she hit the wall, knocking her skull on the rock. A sharp pain shot across her head, and the world spun. Her legs became jelly, and she collapsed, except Silvo still had her arm in his hand.

He dragged her over the floor and down the soldier's tunnel to the main cavern. "You should be proud," he said. "You're going to be the first female of the new king's harem."

Her knees scraped on the rock floor. "You're only the army leader, not the king, dumbass."

Without missing a step, he slammed her against the wall again, her shoulder and hip taking the brunt of the pain.

"That old male's time has come. He hasn't been worth dragon shit since his mate died. And his son is no better, allowing the laws to be broken. The warriors have grown soft under him. That will end as soon as I take over as military leader and king."

She finally gained balance on her feet, then he ascended the stairs toward the archway bedrooms, and she was back to her knees. He hauled her up, her body slapping against each rock step edge. It would've probably hurt if the thumping agony in her head hadn't overpowered everything else.

She reached up and scraped her nails down his forearm. "Let go of me, you dick."

He stopped on the walkway in front of the sleeping rooms that led around the upper cavern wall. Not seeing it coming, Lilah wasn't able to deflect any of the fist that smashed the side of her face.

Before she passed out, she heard him say, "Let the fucking begin."

CHAPTER TWENTY-SIX

Ferrus paced the throne room, anxious to get this over with. He knew his mate would not be harmed with him beside her, but he could not help but worry. He was a warrior trained to fight his way through anything. He had little experience using words. Could his mate pull this off?

He sighed. What was taking his father so long? He marched to the wall to his private rooms and knocked. "My King, I am here." When getting no reply, he knocked again. "The females are bringing down food for you, sire." Still no response. Was his father injured?

Opening the wall, he peeked in. Not seeing anyone, he crossed the living space to the bedroom and knocked. Silence. Fear shot through him. Where was his father? He hurried into the empty throne room. He realized his father had to be in the eating room with all the men waiting for food. He would give him a few more moments until joining them.

Dragon shit! He needed to control his fear. Never before had he any real reason to be frightened. He was the prince and the strongest among the Citogen. His men were the top warriors and could not be defeated. He had nothing else he cared for. That had all changed now. His little mate had brought out more emotions than he knew existed in a fae. He certainly was not ready to handle them all.

His father limped through the entrance from the females' tunnel to the top. Behind him were several of his warriors dressed in battle gear. Why were they here? The main entrance to the throne room opened, and more soldiers filed in, ready to fight.

"What is going on here?" he asked. "Why are they prepared for battle?" The king hobbled past him. "What happened to you? Are you hurt?" Ferrus swiftly went to his father's side.

"Get away from me," the royal growled. Ferrus

backed a step, not believing the treatment from his father. The old man had been angry before, but never like this. Had he known that this strike would have caused his father so much grief, he would have acted differently to make it easier for him.

The soldiers filled the room around the throne. Again, he asked, "Why are my men armed when only you and I are in here? Do they think I would hurt my own father?" He looked around at all the stone-cold faces. Just like he had taught them.

The king sat in his seat, sitting very slowly. "First off, Ferrus, they are no longer *your* men."

"What?" When he made a quick step toward the king, several swords swung toward him, stopping his progress. Fury roiled through him. Never had he expected his males to attack him. "Tell me what has happened." His breaths had become shallow and fast. He was losing his patience.

"Silvo, the new leader, expressed his concern about laws that you allowed to be broken."

"What the demon's hell are you talking about?"

"Mates being together!" His father leaned forward, his face twisted with anger.

All right, he had had enough of this mate issue. "What is your problem with two fae who were born for each other being together? What is so goddess-awful about that?"

His father sat back in his opulent chair. "I tried to save you from my fate, but you refused to follow the rules. Since it is early on, I hope your suffering is not as cruel as mine has been."

Ferrus's mind spun, trying to put together the pieces his father was giving him. The problem was there weren't enough of them. What had his father suffered? The man had grieved his mate, his mother, after she died but…Where was Lilah?

He turned toward the exit, but more swords blocked his path. He stared into the eyes of his men around him. "Do you understand what is going on? My mate and I are fighting for your right to be open with your mates. You will no longer have to hide or be together in secret. You can show your love for each other."

The king snorted.

Ferrus continued. "If you stop me right now, you are severing you and your mate's connections. You will never be together or see each other after this. Silvo has made sure of that. Is that what you want?"

Behind him the king hollered out, "Guards, restrain him."

Before anyone moved, a powerful high-pitched squelch tore through the room. The younger soldiers covered their ears while the older ones stood, shocked. Ferrus couldn't believe it himself. The warning had never been used after he was born.

They were under attack.

Training kicked in, and Ferrus ordered his men to location one, which was to protect all entrances into the mountain. He had to find out what was happening to better plan the next move. But he couldn't do that. He had to find his mate. But if his army fell before he could, they would be prisoners of the enemy.

Since Silvo was not in the room, he could only surmise the Kappie dick had his Lili. But where? He ran with his men to the main cavern where the guard who was outside when Ferrus arrived entered.

"Frontal assault. From the forest."

"Location two," Ferrus roared, borrowing power from his dragon. Everyone would move to the woodland side of the ridge. Something caught his attention. He turned to see Silvo closing the rock wall to one of the archways. His dragon knew as he did that their mate was in there too.

With strength he didn't know he had, Ferrus leapt from the cavern floor to the walkway that was at least ten males' heights up. He landed and fell against the wall creating a crack that webbed out. Throwing the rock door to the side, he prepared to grab Silvo and break his neck. He was not prepared for the surprise attack.

When Ferrus stepped inside, Silvo was tucked to the side wall, already swinging his sword toward his head. With animal-like reflexes, Ferrus went to his knees, the weapon passing harmlessly above him. He surged forward to hold Silvo to the wall, but the fae kicked out, planting his foot in Ferrus's stomach.

Ferrus stumbled back, crashing into the wall, shaking the room if that was possible. His mate lay on the softened rock bed, where she raised her hand to her head and groaned.

"Lili," he called.

"Ferrus?" She tried to sit up but fell sideways. "What's happening?"

Silvo charged the prince with his sword held high. His face was dark red and twisted with hate. Ferrus sat against the wall where he fell, fingers sunk into the rock floor. Fisting a handful of stone, he crushed it into powder.

"Better watch what you are doing, warrior," Ferrus said. His words slowed Silvo's attack, throwing the fae off just enough for Ferrus to throw the rock dust into his eyes. The soldier stumbled back with a growl, rubbing his face.

Using the opportunity, Ferrus rushed to Lilah's side. He helped her to sit up. "How badly are you hurt, my love?"

"Probably a concussion, but I'll be fine. Take care of him." He glanced up at Silvo, eyes redder than normal and watering.

"How charming," Silvo sneered. "You've found your mate. What would your father think of that? He'd have her killed on the spot. And as the army leader, I'd be the one to do it." Instead of going for Ferrus, Silvo leaped to the side, swinging his sword toward Lilah.

Ferrus grabbed her shoulders and slung her to the other side of the soft rock. She bounced and rolled onto the floor close to the entrance.

Ferrus dove away from the bludgeon, popping up onto his knees. "Lilah, get out of here," Ferrus yelled out. For once, she followed his order and disappeared onto the walkway and around the corner.

Silvo advanced in the small space. "She matters

little, Prince. I will take care of her in the harem with the other women when I am king."

Ferrus shook his head. "There always was something off about you, Silvo. Too bad you were such a good fighter. I should've left you as a perimeter guard on the peak."

"Ferrus," he heard his mate call. "Catch." A dark, long pipe flipped end over end, barely missing Silvo. Ferrus caught it and realized it was a metal stick. Where had she gotten that?

Silvo slashed his sword through the air, and Ferrus held his new tool on both ends and blocked the blade. Spark flew from the contact point. From there, he switched his weight to his other foot and kicked his attacker in the midsection. Silvo was thrust back but kept his sword. Time to change sides of the playing field.

Pushing off the wall, Ferrus began his own attack, whipping the pipe around and around, beating on the enemy weapon as the warrior could do nothing but defend himself from the barrage. As they reached the entrance, a plan came into focus. Now, if only his mate didn't have a plan of her own to mess it all up. What were the odds of that happening?

CHAPTER TWENTY-SEVEN

On the walkway outside of the bedroom, Lilah tried to think of something else she could do to help Ferrus. She'd already made a tube of rock and turned it into metal, so he at least had some means to protect himself.

Suddenly, the fighting had changed. Instead of *whooshes* from a blade, one piece of metal was beating the shit out of the other one. Hoping Ferrus was doing the damage, Lilah peeked in and saw her mate driving the prick back out of the room.

Bam. Bam. Bam.

Silvo barely defended himself with his bent and broken weapon.

As her attacker stepped farther toward the outside walkway, she had an idea. Quickly making another rock tube a couple feet longer than the one she forged for her mate, she made a slender pole. Reminded her of a broomstick, minus the broom.

Seconds later, Silvo appeared, sword held above his head to catch the blows from her mate. She scooted toward the edge, praying she wouldn't fall off with this plan of hers. She'd risk it for her mate, the only man she'd ever love.

Silvo was hunched in the middle of the path. Ferrus stepped out of the room and saw her on her knees. Ferrus's attention on her, Silvo leaned back to swing his weapon forward. She was waiting for just this moment. The pipe secure in her hand, Lilah whipped her arms around and landed the bar on the back of the prick's knees.

Caught off guard, Silvo's legs bent, and he fell backward, hitting the edge of the walkway and rolling off. She couldn't watch him hit the ground at least fifty feet below. That was just too gruesome. Didn't matter. Ferrus dragged her to him and scooped her up.

He held her so tightly, she couldn't breathe. Arms around his neck, she didn't care. She needed him more than breath, for the next ten seconds, anyway, until she had to inhale.

The world around her began to seep into her consciousness. Men were running and screaming to the cave entrance.

"What's going on?" she asked, her lips brushing his neck. He shivered.

"We're being attacked," he said like he was asking her if she wanted a drink. The memory of the village elders from earlier in the day popped into her head. They were angry enough with the treatment of the mountain women that they were willing to wage war for them. And who usually headed up such battles? The alphas, Iridia, Zee, and Wren.

"Oh my god, Ferrus. You have to stop this. That's my cousin out there. They can't kill her." She took off running, clinging as close to the wall as she could to not fall off the edge. They really needed to put a railing up. A big, strong railing. Telephone pole big.

Why were the Gnoleons attacking anyway? Did they not think she could handle this? They hadn't given her enough time to accomplish anything.

Ferrus lifted her off her feet, and they sped fae fast to the outside. When he set her down, she scanned the area for one of the alphas or someone she recognized. She quickly realized the tree fae were not the enemy.

From the forest at the base of the mountain, hundreds of creatures with long spears raced upward to meet the red fae standing their ground. The beings were about half the size of the men. But where they lacked in size, they made up with numbers. It looked like someone had tipped over an anthill, and all the little creepy crawlies had come running out.

The warriors easily disarmed the enemy of the spears, when the men could reach them. The little buggers ducked under the swinging weapons without missing a step. They needed a golf swing, not an overhead who-can-hit-the-hardest contest.

"I can't believe this," Ferrus said.

"What?"

"We are fighting Kappies."

"Aren't those the short creatures you all laughed about in the throne room when Wren told you about them?"

"Yes," he replied to her smart-ass comment, "you have made your point."

As she watched, the soldiers were quickly being

overrun by the ants; there were just so many of them.

"Ferrus," she heard the waver in her own voice, "this doesn't look good. Is that all the guys?"

A few warriors had fallen, not because of injuries from weapons, but something else. She squinted, shielding her eyes with her hand. That's when she noticed the Kappies were using the spears as a diversion tactic. Their goal was to get close enough to rake their claws on the fae. As soon as they did, they jumped back to avoid the sword coming their way.

"What are they doing? Trying to make our guys bleed to death from scratches?"

"I don't know," Ferrus said, "but whatever it is, they are taking my men down." He grabbed her and bent down to look into her eyes. "Swear to me you will not try to fight these things. If they break through, promise me you will run and stay alive." She started to shake her head. Of course, she wasn't promising that. His eyes became glassy. "Lilah, please. I cannot fight for my home if I don't know you are safe. Promise me you will get to safety now."

What could she do? She was the reason he

wouldn't fight to save his people. No, that couldn't happen.

"I will hide with the women locked in the kitchen."

His brows drew down. "There is so much in that statement I don't understand, but I trust you to go."

She nodded. "I will. Right now." Lilah headed to the tunnel then stopped when she heard the roar. Ferrus had shifted into his scary-ass dragon. She rushed back to the entrance, staying against the wall to see what happened. If the fae won, then there was no reason for her to hide.

The dragon was in the thickest part of the enemy. His tail whipped around, throwing off dozens of Kappies at one time down the side. More and more of the ants came after him, swiping their claws, but against his metal skin, they were useless. Several had climbed his back and were creeping toward his head. His nose and eyes were still vulnerable.

The dragon shook them off only for another bunch to climb on. The men weren't doing much better. The enemy was too fast to catch with heavy metal weapons. The army was going to be defeated.

CHAPTER TWENTY-EIGHT

Ferrus rubbed his eyes, not believing what they showed him. His army of the strongest warriors on the planet was losing to the weakest of creatures. What were those scratches doing? He was sure there was more to it than the simple breaking of the skin.

Standing in the middle of the Kappies in his dragon form, he could see a black haze surrounding all the Kappies. The haze wasn't dark, more smoky, but he had no doubt what it meant; the enemy had dark magic on their side.

His men were falling—no, more like collapsing — everywhere, but the enemy was now losing a great many. After the men analyzed the opponent's fighting style, just like he had taught them, the warriors shifted to a different means of offense. Instead of swinging to take off a head like usual, they thrust the blades forward right into the chest of the Kappie.

The blue of their blood was beginning to paint a picture along the light-colored stone. A horrid image of life lost. And for what reason? Bangar shit, he didn't even know why the Kappies were attacking. He swept his tail around again and launched many of the little ones into the air to smash against the rocks below.

The numbers of the enemy were increasing as fresh troops ran out of the forest. So many of his men were already down. He could only do so much on his own. He wasn't made for this type of battle. This was warfare he never expected. Seemed he was wrong when he said his men were undefeatable.

A male on his knees tried to pull himself up while he shouted to the others. "They are after the females. They want our mates."

Then the most fantastic thing he had ever seen happened before his eyes.

The males began pulling themselves off the ground, blood dripping from every arm and leg, to fight for the ones they loved. Half dead, too weak to lift a sword, his men snared one Kappie after another and snapped their necks.

His father ruled by fear, using death as a consequence of disobeying. Ferrus thought fear made the warriors strong. But seeing this, he realized he and his father had been wrong. Fear was not the strongest force in existence. Love was.

The Kappies noticed many of their brethren on the ground, their heads at an unnatural angle or body parts bashed on the rock below. They began to back down. They were retreating. The soldiers cheered as they crumpled. He shifted back to his fae form and was about to aid his downed warriors when he heard crunching from the trees.

That was the sound of twigs snapping and leaves crushing under the feet of the second wave of Kappies starting up the mountainside.

He and his men had no chance.

————

LILAH WATCHED in horror as man after man began to fall. Without Ferrus in his dragon form, the main cave would've been filled with the enemy by now. There were so many of the damn little things. Ferrus needed more men. But they were all down there fighting. They had to have more manpower. Oh shit. Not manpower. Woman power!

The woman had their slings and rock throwers. With how one of those simple weapons blew up a melon in the village, she had no doubt this would work.

Running through the entrance, then up the tunnel to where the women were locked up, she wondered if the ladies could get out from the rock. What was the purpose behind the king sealing it if the women could just reopen it? Shit, that might be a problem.

Breathing hard, but not dying like she usually would've been after such a hike, she stood at the wall where she thought the crease might be. With her palm, she beat on the rock and yelled for Valori, hoping the fae could hear her. To her surprise, she faintly heard the woman's voice.

"Valori, we need the women to help fight. Can you get out?"

"Undo the magic sealing the rock together, Lilah. Only one with alpha power can do that."

Damn, that did narrow down potential rescuers a bit. "How do I use magic?" She stared at her hands, wiggling her fingers. She wondered if what she'd done before with the rock turning to metal was just a fluke, some freak event that would never happen again for a million years.

She finally heard Valori reply. "We don't know. It just works."

Were they kidding? *It just works.* Oh god, they were screwed. She calmed herself and thought back to how she did the rock magic. In her mind, she imagined what she wanted to happen.

"All righty then, ladies. Here goes nothing." She placed her hand on the rock as far up as she could reach and closed her eyes. In her head, she saw an oversized zipper attached to the wall. All she had to do was unzip it. Her fingers wrapped around the huge pull, and she tugged as hard as she could. The damn thing needed some WD-40.

When her arms couldn't pull any longer, she was only halfway down. Dammit. There wasn't time for this kind of shit. Still grasping the piece of metal, she lifted her feet, and the unruly zipper teeth began to separate again. Huh, this would be the only time in her life that she wished she weighed more.

When her ass touched the floor, that was as far as she could go. "Valori, try to open it."

A hair-sized ray of sunlight shined through. The one torch way down by the dining room was rather useless, but her eyes had adjusted not having any problems. The beam grew wider 'till the wall split into halves. One side pulled away from the other down to the point where her hand pressed against the rock. It was more of a tall window than a door, but it just worked.

Valori was the first out. Lilah explained what was happening as the women hurried down the tunnel.

"You can use your slings and rocks to pop these little shits' heads like a watermelon hitting concrete from fifty feet up."

They were back to torch light as the source of illumination not far from the side entrance to the throne room when she heard the king yelling. Out of the wall opening into their tunnel, a Kappie slid to a stop. Seeing them, it lifted its claws and hissed.

"Back up," Lilah warned even though they were twenty feet away. "Valori, is the king safe?" she asked, worried the Kappy injured him somehow.

"His Royal Highness is an alpha. He can take care of himself."

"Why isn't he out fighting. Isn't that what a good ruler should do?" Was the bastard a big chicken shit?

"The warrior leader is responsible for leading

the males into battle. The king must stay locked in his rooms. He's old, too, but don't tell him I said that."

The Kappie swiped his claws through the air as it stepped backward. If it meant to scare her, it worked. "There's something bad with those sharp-ass nails," Lilah whispered.

"It's dark magic," Valori replied. "I can see it pulsing around its body, especially his hand."

Before Lilah could ask what they should do, the Kappie exploded. Yes, exploded. She was going to puke after the shock wore off.

"Good job, everyone," Valori said, starting forward. "These Kappies won't be too much of a problem."

Lilah glanced over her shoulder to see half the women with slings in their hands. Together they had destroyed the creature. She saw hands reach out to the walls and snatch out fist-size chunks.

The Kappies had no fucking idea what was coming their way.

CHAPTER TWENTY-NINE

F errus stared at the mass of the enemy hiking the mountainside. They were like insects on the forest floor scuttling over and around each other. It seemed their intent was to take down his warriors, lessen their numbers. Where was their cowardly leader? Not at the front where a true leader should be.

He went to the male closest to him on the ground and looked over his wounds. Scratch marks sliced his man's skin in several places. From each gouge, a black line had slithered under the flesh, worming its way up the arm or leg. It was if a parasite had invaded the body and was digging in, leaving a trail.

He'd never seen this before. As far as he knew, they had no medicine for this type of injury.

"Does it hurt?" he asked.

"I feel it in me," the soldier replied. "It's cold and seeking my soul. It wants to kill my magic." His eyes closed, breathing becoming shallower.

"Fight it, Fusecut," Ferrus instructed. "Your mate is expecting you tonight."

A growl came from the fae's chest, his eyes opening. Through clenched teeth, he said, "I will see her again. The enemy inside will not destroy me."

Ferrus squeezed the soldier's shoulder. "Be strong, warrior."

When he pulled away, his man grabbed his arm. "Ferrus, know that we didn't want to follow the orders of the king to imprison you. You have trained us not only to fight but to think. We would not have let Silvo or the king harm you or your mate in any way. We would fight to the death for you. You are in our hearts."

Emotions he didn't understand coursed through him. These men believed in him, trusted him, would die for him. He realized he would do the same for them. Which was appropriate since time had run out. Ferrus shifted into his dragon once again. To defend his home and fae, knocking many of the Kappies down the rocky slopes.

They came at him and his remaining men in a wave of green and brown. Their claws had no effect on him as they could not penetrate his metal armor. He might be the only survivor at the end of this.

As he waited for the first Kappie to strike, that creature suddenly flew backward, taking several of his fellow fighters with him. Then another jerked back off its feet. And another and another. What was happening?

When a sharp sting hit his back, he glanced up the slope to see the females in a line, twirling their slings at their sides and launching rocks. A wall of small but deadly projectiles whizzed by him. Not wanting to be a rock block, he lay flat, using his tail to smack back any enemy who happened to make it that far.

Many men looked on in awe as the "useless" females, who couldn't fight for their home, held in check the marauders who would take all his fae had. He saw his pale-skinned beauty standing behind the females, helping to create ammunition for the slings.

His heart swelled with pride. His mate was now

a warrior queen, able to not only provide for her people but protect her home. He knew sometime soon, they had to decide whether to stay or flee from his father's persecution.

Kappies tumbled over themselves, dragging the militia farther down the mountain. The females advanced forward, quickly reaching some of the downed males. He shifted to catch his mate as she slid down the loose ground to get to him.

"Lili, my goddess, I love you. But I will have to spank you for breaking your promise to me."

Her arms tightened around his neck. "Do you see me lifting a finger against these little shits?" He chuckled. She was right. She technically wasn't fighting anyone. She kissed his cheek and whispered, "But you can still spank me if you want."

His body went up in flame. Damnation! What this woman could do to him. She pulled back, glancing down the mountainside. "Ferrus, keep fighting. I'll see if we can help the injured men." She yanked him down for a burning kiss. "Don't die on me. I love you."

CHAPTER THIRTY

And love him, she did, with all her soul. Not only did he prove he would stay by her, but that she was worthy of having love despite the hurtful words others had said to her. All she had to do was find the group she belonged with, and now that she had, she'd find true happiness and acceptance.

She searched the battleground for Valori and found her kneeling beside an older soldier with blood covering his body. The tenderness on the elder female's face surprised her. Holding the matriarchal position, Val never let herself become soft. If she did, she wouldn't have been able to protect her women as well as she had.

Lilah ran over to join her.

"Alpha female," Val said, "this is my mate, Fusecut."

Shocked, Lilah stared at the man. Of course, the older woman had a mate. Why wouldn't she? Valori just seemed so put together, too serious to have a mate. "Nice to meet you," Lilah said.

"It's my honor, Alpha. You are worthy of great devotion, as is your mate."

Hells bells. Which mate did he mean? The one by nature or the one she'd chosen? Had to be Ferrus. Silvo was dead.

"Thank you, Fusecut," she replied, then smiled. "Let's see if we can get you patched up." She glanced at Ferrus in his dragon form, holding the enemy back with assistance from the women, so she could safely work. "What do we need to make the men better?"

Valori bent lower over her mate. "I've never seen this injury before. It is surely dark magic winding its way to his source of magic."

"Source of magic?" Lilah didn't know there was such a thing.

Valori placed a hand on her chest. "Magic comes from the heart, Alpha. The heart holds the two strongest forces in nature, magic and love."

Boy, she had a lot to learn. "Okay," she replied, "how do we use those to heal your mate?"

The elder's face paled. "I don't know. This is different from anything we've experienced."

Oh, fabulous. Was this going to be another *it just works* deal? She let out a deep breath and put her brain to work. A memory from the time they were in the village came to mind. "Valori, you said the rock is essential to your lives."

"Yes, Alpha. We are made of it and will return to it when the Mother of the Mountain decides it is time."

"Well," Lilah said more to herself, "if it acts like stem cells for humans, let's see if it will do miraculous things too."

Lilah scooped up a chunk of rock and crushed it in her hand. She rubbed the dust over several scratches and examined the results. As the blood soaked up the powder, the combination settled deeper into the cuts. A spark flew up as a small flame disappeared under the skin. The base of the dark lines from those scratches that had webbed through every vein in his arm turned red then vanished.

Fusecut screamed and grabbed for his arm, but

with Valori's help, she restrained him. Valori gasped. "How do you know this?"

Lilah shrugged a shoulder. "It just works." She glanced up at Valori staring at her, and they smiled. Turning her attention back to Val's mate, Lilah noticed the fire that was eating the dark magic in Fusecut's veins began to slow then stopped.

"Why isn't it working," Lilah asked. She thought she had it figured out.

"It is not strong enough," Valori guessed.

"How do you make rock stronger?" The question was rhetorical, but Lilah said it anyway out of frustration.

"Yes, Muriel, go," Val said. Lilah looked up to see the elder talking to someone behind Lilah. Then the young lady who made the beautiful sword hilts at the lava river darted up the slope. Before Lilah could ask, Val explained. "We have discovered that the leftover ash from burning metal out of the rock to make weapons has several beneficial uses."

Lilah remembered Val saying the kitchen knives were higher quality than the soldier's weapons because Muriel added ash to the mix when she made them.

"Just recently," Val said, "we discovered that putting ash on the garden soil produces bigger and more crops."

"Got it," Lilah nodded. "You're hoping the ash mixed with the rock dust will be enough to eat all the dark magic." When she said those words, she felt in her bones that this was the solution to the cure. She jumped to her feet. "I've been to the mine. I'll help Muriel bring ash up."

Lilah dashed through the entrance into the big cavern where the arched bedrooms and most of the daily chores were done. She looked around and realized she didn't know how to get to the right tunnel from here. When she and Daph stumbled upon it, they had come from the kitchen.

Shit. The only way to be sure was to get to the corridor that went past the throne room. From here to get to the king's chamber was easy. In a fast jog, she headed along the path. Approaching the double doors with the magnificent dragon on it—which now made sense to her seeing that Ferrus was a dragon—she saw a body slumped to the floor. Was that the guard who stood at the doors?

Reaching the throne entrance, she checked for a pulse on the fae, not knowing if they even had one. Feeling nothing, she focused on the voices from inside the room and quickly peeked in. Inside, she saw Silvo—bruised and battered— arguing with the king outside the entrance to his chambers. Luckily, Silvo's back was to her. The king was saying something about the "three females" and capturing them.

Of course, that was why the Kappies were attacking. They knew she and her cousins were here. That scout they saw when first climbing the mountain path must have seen them. Shit. All this was because of her and the portal rocks.

Those two could fight out whatever they want. She needed to get down to the mine. As she turned, she heard the word *dragon*, and the king started screaming. They had to be talking about Ferrus. What other dragon was there?

She leaned to the side just enough for her eyes to see past the door's edge. The king had gotten in Silvo's face and was yelling about respecting royalty. Silvo slowly slid his hand around to his backside, fingers grabbing something at his waistband. A flash reflected off the item, and she knew what it was, one of the female's knives.

Before she could shout a warning to the king, Silvo swung his arm around and slashed the king's throat. If that wasn't enough, he stabbed the king in the chest. When his hand raised for another slice, she was unable to stop the gasp from the horrific scene.

Silvo looked over his shoulder and locked eyes with hers. Panic taking over, Lilah sprinted back toward the cavern. How the hell had Silvo survived that fall from the walkway? Apparently, the fae were harder to kill than humans. For the king's sake, she hoped they were very hard to kill.

Slapping footsteps gaining on her, she put more speed on, her thigh muscles responding to the demand. As she ran, she half expected a piercing burn in her back where the kitchen knife would sink into her. Instead, she jerked to a stop when the asshole grabbed the back of her shirt.

He slammed her against the wall, and her body throbbed as she plunged to the floor. As he dragged her, he laughed. "I believe we've done this before."

She tried to rip the skin from his arm like she had when he attacked her the first time, but he was wise to that stunt and held her at a different angle. Stopping in the cavern, Silvo pulled her up and placed the edge of the bloody knife on her throat.

"Listen and obey me, and you might live." She doubted that at this point but kept her mouth shut.

Yay for her. "We are going down another tunnel, and I want you to walk in front of me. If you do anything besides walk, this knife will take your head off."

He shoved her down the passage that led to the holding cells. He was going to lock her up. That was fine. He didn't know she could bend the bars like they were spaghetti noodles. Then she could escape out the secret door at the end of the tunnel. The same exit the women used when sneaking out before the strike.

"I can't believe you killed your own father," she said. "Such a good son, you are."

"What are you talking about? I'm not the king's worthless son. He'll be next to fall by my hand very soon."

Wait, what? Who was the prince then? Could it be... Now it made sense that the mating call was right. Oh god. She was so stupid. How did she not see it? Love was truly blind and dumb.

When reaching the opening for the prison, Silvo growled. "Keep going."

Her optimism vanished. They were going someplace else. Possibly out the same secret opening? When they reached the dead-end wall, Silvo kept her in front of him as he pulled apart the rock. Once again, at the mountain's base, she saw the enemy among the trees. There were even more of these little shits. God help them.

Silvo pushed her out, wrapping his large hand around her neck. His fingers rested on her windpipe, which he could no doubt crush.

He yelled a name she'd never heard. "Luzzeh. Luzzeh Full. I'm here to make a bargain that you'll want." They waited until a guy wearing animal fur around his body stepped out and came to them.

"I am Luzzeh, King of the trolls in the Crystal Kingdom, now the ruler of the Kappie population. What deal would I *want* to make with you?"

Silvo pushed her forward a step. "This is one of the females you are searching for. A daughter, perhaps."

Lilah twisted her neck around enough to see the dumbass's face. "What? Are you joking? Do I look anything like him? I don't think so."

Luzzeh smiled. "I haven't seen this one, but yes, by her clothes and words, she is one of the three I seek. What do you want for her?"

"I want your dark magic to kill that dragon."

He meant Ferrus. Anger raced through her. She pivoted her body and kicked for the jerk's balls, but he moved, so she hit his thigh. His hand tightened around her neck until she felt her throat push against her windpipe. She stopped struggling, sucking in as much air as she could.

"I don't necessarily need her," Luzzeh said. "I want the stone she carries. After I get that, you can kill her. Search her pockets."

Silvo dragged her back against his body. He leaned down and licked her cheek. "I'll gladly feel all her pockets." His hand slid down her stomach, headed directly south when her pocket was more southeast. Disgust rolled through her as she anticipated his touch on her girly parts.

Not able to take it, she turned her lower body to the side and dug into her pocket to pull out the gemstone Grandmom had given them to open a portal back to Earth.

"Here," she said, "just take it." Silvo was going to find it no matter what, and this way, she at least avoid wandering hands. She held it out on her palm. Luzzeh pulled a drawstring bag from his waist and held it open.

"Drop it in here."

Damn this moment. There was only one thing she could do. She hoped she wouldn't condemn her and her cousins to a life of hell in this dimension. She closed her fingers around the stone, then slowly put her fist in the bag and let the stone fall in. Her hand came out open and empty. Luzzeh closed the bag, tucking it into his belt.

"Now kill the dragon," Silvo snarled, throwing her to the ground, forgetting about her.

Luzzeh scoffed. "I want all three of the females before I do what you want."

"That wasn't the deal." Silvo stepped forward and squeezed Luzzeh's throat. "I will kill you if you don't obey me."

Then something strange happened. A smoky shadowlike fog rolled off the Kappie King's neck, up the warrior's arm, and into his chest. Silvo inhaled a deep breath, and his eyes turned red for a couple seconds. Then a roar ripped out of him that shook the ground.

He laughed hysterically, just like the Joker in Batman. Whoever laughed that kind of laugh couldn't be a good person. Silvo turned his palms up and stared at his hands.

"This feels great. So much power."

Lilah glanced at a wide-eyed Luzzeh. "Did he just take your magic?" she asked. Was that even possible? Between his hands, Silvo created a ball of something—energy or dark magic and launched it toward the mountain. In a few second's time, the ball slammed into Ferrus's dragon form. The Kappies surrounding him blew away like leaves in the wind.

Holy shit. How did he do that? Ferrus roared, falling onto his side. Silvo lifted his hands to make another ball, but he wasn't going to throw it.

Lilah attacked. She gave him a kidney punch in the back, hoping fae had kidneys or some vital organ there. Silvo bent backward, his head going back as another roar ripped from him. Next, she went for his knees, trying to kick them forward so he'd fall, anything to keep him from hurting her mate again.

His one leg curved, but it did little to stop the backhand that slammed into her face, taking her down. Her world spun as pain and heat sliced across her head. She could barely move without her stomach revolting.

"Stay out of my way, female. You will soon have enough of me after I chain you down and fuck you time and time again."

Silvo threw another circle of magic. She couldn't see where it was going, but Ferrus's agonizing roar ripped her heart open. High-pitched screams filled the air as the Kappies retreated down the hill, running from the killing magic.

Silvo did that stupid laugh again. She had to stop him the only way she knew how. She reached out and touched his shoe with a fingertip, imagining his whole body as a bronze statue on a pedestal in front of a building.

Silvo's laugh turned into a terror-filled scream. Luzzeh lunged toward him, arms out, and the dark magic jumped back to him. It must've sensed the oncoming transformation of a living organism into cold, hard metal.

Then her world slipped into pain-free darkness.

CHAPTER THIRTY-ONE

Lying on the rocky slope in his dragon form, Ferrus waited for the next and final shot of dark magic to rip through him, destroying his body and mind. Screams from the Kappies were all around him as they ran around in chaos.

He heard his name, and Valori slid to a stop beside his snout. "Ferrus." He opened his eyes. "Thank the goddess of the mountain you are alive. How badly injured are you?"

He didn't care about his physical well-being at the moment. He needed to know his mate was safe. Changing to his fae form, the damaged muscles, bones, and organs regenerated to heal all the effects of the dark magic on him. He lay on his side, panting like he had run up the entire mountain nonstop.

"Where is Lilah?" he said between breaths.

The elder's smile melted away. "We are searching for her."

He pushed himself to sit up. "Searching?"

Shinni popped out of the entrance. "Prince, come quickly, the King is dying." What? His mind tumbled around, trying to understand all that was happening. Last he knew, they were losing the battle against a horde of Kappies. Where had they gone?

Valori grabbed his arm and pulled him up. "Ferrus, you must go to the throne room now." She half dragged him inside until things cleared, and he could think again. Whatever had hit him messed him up badly. He heard the words again: the King is dying.

He snapped to attention then ran with fae speed through the tunnels to find his father on the floor outside the entrance to his rooms. Several fae in the room were kneeling and crying. Around his father's shoulders, his blood had pooled.

Ferrus knelt and placed his hands on the King's forehead and chest. "Father, change into your alpha dragon and heal yourself." Like him, his father had a dragon inside that had lain dormant for hundreds of peaks.

His father breathed out, "Ferrus."

The prince lowered his ear to the king's mouth. "I am here, Father. Transform before you die."

"Ferrus," whispered the king, "I tried to save you from the pain of losing a mate, but I was wrong. Wrong about so many things. When your mother died, the father you knew died with her. I could not stand seeing our fae with their mates and happy, knowing I could never see my only love again. I forbade mates, Ferrus, out of envy. Out of grief. Do not let it continue."

"Rest, Father, while we heal you." He glanced up. "Valori, please." The elder pushed through the room full of fae to his side. She sprinkled a dusty mixture in a bowl onto his wounds.

"It is too late for me, my son. I wish to go to the place your mother exists. I want to hold her in my arms again and tell her I love her. I have missed her so much, son."

To his surprise, his sister's presence calmed him. "Father," Ferra said, "go freely to where the sun always shines on you, and the rock is soft under your feet. You have raised an upright and brave heir to make sure we will continue to grow strong. Rest with peace, Father."

"Thank you, daughter. Find your mate and be happy always." His eyes rolled to meet Ferrus's tearful ones. "Same for you, son. Be happy with your mate always—"

The King's eyes closed, and his chest became still.

CHAPTER THIRTY-TWO

When Lilah woke, she stared up at a stone ceiling. Not her canopy bed at home. She wasn't sure if she was happy or sad at that. No, she took back that thought. She was happy. The love of her life lived within these rock walls, and she wanted to be with him. Last she remembered, Silvo was about to kill him with dark magic.

She bolted straight up in a bed and looked around. In the room around her, several men lay on softened-rock beds sleeping. They each scratches covering their body, but those scrapes were covered with a gray powder that she assumed was a mix of rock and ash.

"She's awake!" came from the entrance of the

cave room they were in. From there, those words echoed out, but with different voices until the sound faded away. They really needed to find a way to communicate other than hollering.

From around the corner of the entrance, Ferrus slid into view like Tom Cruise wearing tighty whities in Risky Business. Behind him came Daphne and Wren and Zee. Wow, you'd think she'd been out for a year or something. Well, she hoped she hadn't.

Ferrus cupped her face in his hands and kissed her long and hard. When he pulled back, he rested his forehead on hers.

"Goddess, you had me worried," he whispered. "How do you feel?"

She did a mental check of her body. "I feel fine. Nothing hurts. How long have I been out?"

"Overnight," Daphne answered. "We were attacked yesterday."

Everything came back to her. She checked to make sure she was clothed before flipping off the blanket. "Can I get up? I'm hungry."

"As long as you feel fine, why not?" Daphne replied, helping her with the blanket. Taking Ferrus's hand, she stood, still feeling normal. They walked out to a busy cavern. She hadn't seen it like this.

"What's going on?" she asked.

"Out here, we're digging out more sleep coves, so there is less sharing," Ferrus replied.

"Great," she said. "How did the men react to the change when you told them?"

He frowned. "There was a grumble or two, but only from the unmated fae."

"They'll get over it," Daphne added. Yes, the men would have to grow up.

Ferrus asked, "What else do we need to do?" They turned up the tunnel the men used to get to the dining cave.

Lilah brightened with energy. "There are so many things I'd love to do. First off, Muriel can teach some of the men how to turn the rough stone walls and ceilings into beautiful stone artwork like the Romans. I want to put mirrors throughout and get the sunlight down here. I want to expand the mates' rooms. I thought maybe the children would like to visit and stay over with their parents. Then…"

Ferrus laughed. "Slow down, my love. I hope you don't plan on this all happening overnight."

"Well, no," she answered. "It'll take some time, but we can get it done."

Leading the group, Daphne stopped in the middle of the tunnel. "Lilah, you make it sound like you're staying. We have to go home."

The insight hit her hard. Thinking back, she realized she'd always seen herself as staying. Learning everyone's names, learning the culture. And she couldn't leave the love of her life.

She turned her eyes to her mate. "Daph, I don't think I can leave. Ferrus's people need him right now, and I'm not going anywhere without him. I have to make sure the changes for the women go as smoothly as possible. If that means social skills and harassment training for the men, I will need to do that. Someone has to write a bill of rights and new laws to govern the people. I thought about setting up test groups and a way for others to make a complaint anonymously."

"I get it," Daphne said. "But what do we tell Grandmom?"

"She's a princess," Wren said. "If anyone understands what makes a good leader, it's her. She can visit anytime she wants. So can we, right?" Wren raised a brow at Ferrus.

"Absolutely," he fumbled the word trying to get it out fast enough. "Always."

Daphne nodded and continued up the slope silently. Lilah wondered if her cousin was genuinely upset that she wanted to stay. It wasn't like she had been overly nice to Daphne. Guilt ate at her, thinking back to some of the things she'd said to her best friend.

"Hey, Daph." Lilah reached out and snagged Daph's hand to stop them again. "I want to apologize to you for the way I've treated you for a long time."

Daphne looked away. "No. I'm okay—"

"No," Lilah interjected, "I want to say this. When we were growing up, I was so jealous of you. My mom wanted me to be like you. She saw you as the perfect daughter. Then you and Wren together...You both were so brave climbing trees and racing your bikes. Because of my weight, I was afraid to do those things. I always wanted to look like you, tall and thin. You're so graceful, Daph. You never trip over your own feet."

Wren added, "That's for sure. You were always the best in ballet class."

"But—" Daph started.

"Let me finish," Lilah said. She had to get all of

this out now. "I've let my insecurities rule how I treated you, and I'm sorry I was a bitch so many times to you. You both stood by me all these years, and I'm grateful." She reached back for Wren's hand. "You two have always been more than just cousins to me. Next to Ferrus, you two mean everything to me." She sniffled, trying unsuccessfully to keep the stupid tears at bay.

Daphne hugged her. "Apology accepted," she said, "though none was really needed. Even when I hated you for being bitchy, I still loved you. You're family, Lil. Both of you are." Wren joined in for a group hug. Just like when they were kids, and it was them against the world.

Wren murmured in her ear, "Don't worry about Grandmom or your family. Daph and I will handle them all. Just hold on to your gemstone, so you have it when you want to come home."

Oh shit. She forgot about the portal stone. She'd given it to the Kappie leader. Well, she gave Luzzeh a lump of metal. No telling if it still worked or not. She doubted he'd try it.

"Yeah, have Grandmom come visit anyway. You know, in case I lose my rock or something." They all laughed.

"We will all visit you. Probably more than you

want." Wren glanced at Ferrus, then winked at her. Oh, there would be no shortage of sex in her future.

After a long moment, Lilah's grouchy stomach got the best of her. "Okay, I'm still hungry." She snapped her fingers. "Daph, lead the way."

With Ferrus, Lilah dropped behind Wren and Zee. He whispered, "You are amazing, Lili. I love you so much. You're going to be a great queen."

She stopped and gave him the stink eye, fists on her hips. "And when were you planning on telling me *you* are the prince?" At least he had the decency look guilty.

"I thought you knew."

She threw her arms into the air. "And who would've told me? Nobody bowed to you that I saw or called you the prince that I heard." Many other clues that simply didn't click.

"Don't worry, love," Ferrus said, his smile became devious. "Tonight, I will kneel at your feet and prove to you I'm your king while you're screaming my name."

"Why wait until tonight? We're really not needed right now. Show me to your room, mate." Lilah grinned and tugged him down the passage. She knew he would take the lead and not allow her to get lost.

He swooped down and kissed her hard. He slipped his tongue between her lips, slowly claiming every crevice of her mouth. Ferrus picked her up, and she wrapped her legs around his hips.

He groaned, cupping the heavy mounds of her breasts in his hands and thumbing her nipples. "These are so beautiful." Her blood sizzled as electricity traveled from her nipples to her clit. She moaned.

"Yes," she groaned, sliding her fingers into Ferrus's hair. His lips split into a sinful smile.

Ferrus carried her into a room and laid her on another soft rock pallet. She didn't take the time to look around his room. There would be plenty of time for that later.

He sucked her nipples, biting down and leaving them wet stinging points. He

slid a hand down, cupped her pussy, slid a finger between her pussy lips to her entrance, and then up to her clit. "You're so wet. Slick and hot."

Ferrus let go of her body to strip off his clothing.

Her blood sizzled in her veins. Dots of sweat gathered over her skin. Ferrus slipped between her legs, coming around on his knees to face her pussy.

He lifted her thigh over his shoulder. Her leg shook from his breath between her legs. He ran a finger over her folds.

"I can't wait to taste you," he said, gliding his finger up and pressing into her pussy. Ferrus fucked her with his finger and licked her clit with his tongue.

He pressed his face into her pussy, flicking circles around her clit. Ferrus sucked her clit into his mouth. Heat traveled up her body, shoving her over the edge and into an explosive release. She screamed; her body shook.

Ferrus grinned up at her from between her legs, and she licked her lips. She panted between heaving breaths, "Flip over, I want to ride you."

She waited until he lay next to her, and she climbed over and straddled him. She didn't hesitate. Instead, she pressed down, taking his cock in one glide. She was wet, soaked from her previous orgasm. She rocked back and forth on his cock.

She wiggled a little as Ferrus lifted his hips and thrust into her pussy. Tension wound tight in her belly. It happened so fast she didn't realize she was coming until she dug her nails into his arms, letting her body unravel while he continued to drive in and out of her.

Lilah screamed as another orgasm shook her body and Ferrus yelled out his release. It was time to make up for lost time over the past few years.

Yum.

EPILOGUE

L uzzeh sat on his throne, staring at his newly acquired artwork. A bronze statue of someone who tried to steal his magic from him.

He had watched as the metal consumed the male from his foot up to his head. It looked rather painful. Luzzeh was giddy from the power of the dark magic he had taken from the fae before his brain turned to metal and died.

That added power tasted mighty fine. He wanted more of it…more fae to drink down. Absolute power the darkness had before the fairy queen interfered would be his. He would devour the light, the fairy queen, then all of Crystal Kingdom in his revenge.

He already had the first stone. He patted the bag tied to his waist belt to feel the hard object inside. Getting the other two wouldn't be difficult. Besides, he knew where the females were going. There was only one place in this damnation dimension where a portal out could be opened.

And, with an army twice the size of what he had now, he would be there waiting for them.

ABOUT THE AUTHOR

New York Times and USA Today Bestselling Author

Hi! I'm Milly Taiden. I love to write sexy stories featuring fun, sassy heroines with curves and growly alpha males with fur. My books are a great way to satisfy your craving for paranormal romance with action, humor, suspense and happily ever afters.

I live in Florida with my hubby, our son, and our fur babies: Speedy, Stormy and Teddy. I have a serious addiction to chocolate and cake.

I love to meet new readers, so come sign up for my newsletter and check out my Facebook page. We always have lots of fun stuff going on there.

SIGN UP FOR MILLY'S NEWSLETTER FOR LATEST NEWS!

http://eepurl.com/pt9q1

Find out more about Milly here:
www.millytaiden.com
milly@millytaiden.com

Alpha Geek

Alpha Geek: *Knox*

Alpha Geek: *Zeke*

Alpha Geek: *Gray*

Alpha Geek: *Brent*

Alpha Geek: *Bennett*

Alpha Geek: *Shaw*

Savage Kiss *Book Two*

Savage Hunger *Book Three*

Savage Caress *Book Four*

ALSO BY MILLY TAIDEN

Drachen Mates

Bound in Flames *Book One*

Bound in Darkness *Book Two*

Bound in Eternity *Book Three*

Bound in Ashes *Book Four*

Federal Paranormal Unit

Wolf Protector *Federal Paranormal Unit Book One*

Dangerous Protector *Federal Paranormal Unit Book Two*

Unwanted Protector *Federal Paranormal Unit Book Three*

Deadly Protector *Federal Paranormal Unit Book Four*

Also, check out the **Paranormal Dating Agency World on Amazon**

Or visit http://mtworldspress.com

ALSO BY MILLY TAIDEN

Sassy Mates / Sassy Ever After Series

Scent of a Mate *Book 1*

A Mate's Bite *Book 2*

Unexpectedly Mated *Book 3*

A Sassy Wedding *Short 4*

The Mate Challenge *Book 5*

Sassy in Diapers *Short 6*

Fighting for Her Mate *Book 7*

A Fang in the Sass *Book 8*

Also, check out the **Sassy Ever After World on Amazon or visit http://mtworldspress.com**

The Alien Warrior's Woman *Book One*

The Alien's Rebel *Book Two*

Other Works

The Hunt

Wynters Captive

Every Witch Way

Hex and Sex Set

Alpha Owned

Match Made in Hell

Wolf Fever

If you enjoyed the book, please consider leaving a review, even if it's only a line or two; it would make all the difference and would be very much appreciated.

Thank you!

Printed in Great Britain
by Amazon